On the other side of the door he could hear the low rumble of voices. Gently, he tried turning the knob.

It was locked. That killed the element of surprise, but with the AK-47 he probably wouldn't need it.

He stood beside the door, flipped the AK-47 on full automatic, and squeezed. Wood shattered and splinters flew.

"Good night, scum," Carter hissed.

NICK CARTER IS IT!

FROM THE NICK CARTER
KILLMASTER SERIES

NICK CARTER

KILLMASTER

Target Red Star

C

CHARTER BOOKS, NEW YORK

TARGET RED STAR

A Charter Book/published by arrangement with
The Condé Nast Publications, Inc.

PRINTING HISTORY
Charter edition/January 1986

ISBN: 0-441-79822-5

Charter Books are published by The Berkley Publishing Group,
200 Madison Avenue, New York, New York 10016.
PRINTED IN THE UNITED STATES OF AMERICA

Dedicated to the men of the
Secret Services of the
United States of America

TARGET RED STAR

ONE

Carter stepped from the taxi into the teeming street and flipped the driver a bill. It was double the fare.

"Keep it."

"*Merci, monsieur, merci.* Go with Allah."

On the curb, Carter lit a cigarette and absorbed the sights, sounds, and smells of Tangier's Boulevard Mohammed V. Through the smoke that spiraled up across his eyes, he checked the street both ways.

Earlier that evening, playing tourist in the Medina, he had thought that he had picked up a tail.

It was improbable, but Nick Carter was always overly cautious. He had to be. Agents of Washington's supersecret AXE were either cautious, or dead.

Satisfied, he stepped across the street and made his way through honking cars and speeding Vespas to the casino. It was an elaborate, mosaic-fronted concoction designed to feed old-world titillation to the tourists, luring them in for the fleecing.

"Your passport, monsieur?"

Carter passed across a United Kingdom passport in the name of Lawrence Hale. There really had been a Lawrence Hale once, many years before. He had died at the age of three months, in Cardiff, Wales.

British intelligence had supplied the passport. It was part of the joint operation between AXE and MI6.

"The main gaming room is right through that door, monsieur."

Carter pocketed his passport and waved the blue admittance tag at the dark-suited little man at the door.

"*Bonne chance, monsieur.*"

"Thank you." A little luck never hurt.

It was a large and ornate room. The whole ceiling was like the inside of a Bedouin tent, and the walls were hung with heavy tapestries. The lighting, except over the gaming tables, was muted. The sound was equally muted, yet intense: the whirr of roulette wheels, the sharp crack of cards, the click of dice, and low conversation in grunted syllables in five languages.

The main room was crowded, mostly around the lower-stake blackjack and roulette tables. But still, there was no shortage of suckers seated at the big-limit wheels and the two baccarat stands.

Carter bought five hundred British pounds' worth of chips and elbowed his way through the milling gamblers, stopping at a particular roulette table. He dropped a five-hundred-dirham chip on black and clicked the others as he continued to scan the room.

And then he saw her—it had to be her—at the second baccarat table. She was hard to miss. He would have spotted her the moment he came through the door, but she was standing instead of sitting at the table, and from the door she had been partially obscured.

Her face was exquisitely beautiful, pale skin surrounded by a mane of honey-blond hair. Her eyes were a greenish-blue, and all the more striking because of an Oriental lift at their corners.

The white satin evening gown she wore hugged every inch of her tall frame, leaving none of its voluptuousness to the imagination.

"Monsieur?"

Carter looked down. The little white ball had dropped on red. He flipped another chip—a thousand-dirham one this time—to the croupier.

"Red."

"*Oui, monsieur. Red.*"

The man sitting directly in front of her was short, slender, with thinning white hair and sagging shoulders. His face and hands sported yellowish, liver-spotted skin. His shoulders seemed shrunken in the expensive cut of the white dinner jacket he wore.

He looked like a tired old millionaire on his last romp.

But Carter knew that was a lie, a carefully cultivated illusion. Hamir Aflag was one of the most powerful arms brokers in the world. He also ran a very profitable sideline in the assassination business, as well as doing a lot of liaison work between the KGB and terrorist representatives of Third World countries.

The woman glanced his way. Carter met her eyes for an instant. Then she raked down his body and returned her gaze to the table.

The look had been short in duration but, Carter knew, long enough for her to make him.

He heard the little white ball drop at his own table, and looked down.

Black.

That's life, he thought, and moved toward the bar, hoping the two losses didn't indicate a complete run of bad luck.

"Whiskey. Chivas. One cube."

"*Oui, monsieur.*"

When the barman returned, Carter asked him the identity of the aristocratic-looking gentleman in the white dinner jacket at the baccarat table.

"A very powerful and rich man, monsieur. His name is Hamir Aflag."

"Oh?" Carter replied, keeping the dumb look on his face. "Actually, I was wondering who the blonde at his shoulder was." A hundred-dirham note floated from his hand to the bar.

"I believe she is Monsieur Aflag's niece," he replied, the note deftly disappearing into his cummerbund.

"Niece for this month, don't you mean?"

The barman coughed into the back of his hand like a good servant. "I wouldn't know about that, monsieur." He drifted away to another customer.

Carter sipped his scotch and studied both the old man and the young woman in the mirror behind the bar. As he watched them, their images began to jiggle, like a mirage. . . .

She was big, almost six feet, blond, and very buxom. Her name was Greta, and she was a secretary in Hamburg. She was wearing a shiny satin robe of a glowing wine-red color. It was pulled tight at the waist by a matching satin sash, but above and below the waist it was loose and carelessly arranged. And it was obvious that she was wearing absolutely nothing under it.

Carter had been romping all afternoon with her on the beach at Marbella, on Spain's Costa del Sol. Finally he had convinced her that dinner with him was absolutely essential. At dinner he convinced her that she should grab some overnight things from her modest hotel room and spend the night in his villa.

"You must be very rich," she said, her fingers idly toying with the barely tied sash. "A villa like this costs a great deal of money."

"I have a very large expense account."

"You are American?"

"Only the passport. Expatriate. Is that important?"

"No. I have a week left of my holiday. We will have a good time, *ja*?"

"Oh, yeah. *Ja*."

His fingers were working at the sash when the phone rang.

"Yeah?" he grunted into the receiver.

"Witten-Jones here. It's a go, old man."

"When?"

"Now."

Carter glanced over his shoulder at Greta. She had dropped the robe herself and was now posed lasciviously, wearing only a bracelet and a smile.

She was a willing Teutonic amazon, the embodiment of every young boy's erotic fantasies, let alone a tired old agent's.

"Now?" Carter rasped.

"Right now, old man. There's a car already waiting for you at the gate to your villa."

The connection was severed, and Greta was all heat and scent in his arms. Her breasts were like two huge feather pillows across his chest, and her buttocks had a life of their own in his hands.

"Let us make love," she breathed.

"I wish I could let us," Carter growled, sure that he was going to melt from the heat of her body. "But I have to go."

"Go?" She jumped back three paces and everything in her body danced. "You leave?"

"I must. Business."

"Bastard!"

"True. But I'll tell you what. Here's some spending money, and the villa is yours for the rest of your vacation. Have a good time on me. I'm sure there's someone around who can keep you . . . er, company."

Leaving her with her chin practically down to her cleavage, he headed for the bedroom.

It had come sooner than any of them had expected. Only two days before, he had been between assignments in D.C. when the call had come from David Hawk, head of AXE.

"We've been working on this one for a long time, N3. For nearly a year we have tried to find some way to put Hamir

Aflag out of business legitimately. It's no deal, no way. So now we have the green light to go wet. About three months ago MI6 infiltrated him with a female agent. All we had to do was wait for the time and place.''

"Where?''

"Somewhere in Morocco. When it's a go, it will be fast . . . in, done, out. I've rented a villa for you near Marbella. Be a playboy until the call comes. Your contact is Sir Richard Witten-Jones.''

Carter thought he would have at least a week, perhaps longer, in the villa.

"Two lousy days," he hissed to himself, throwing what little he had brought into a bag. There wasn't much: spare shirts, socks, underwear, and a bathing suit. The dark suit he had on would soon be discarded, along with everything else. And not a single garment contained a label.

Back in the living room, Greta was already on the phone. As he emerged from the bedroom, she held her hand over the mouthpiece and flashed him a wide, beaming smile.

"You are sure . . . the villa?''

"Sure.''

"I was just calling a . . . girl friend.''

"Sure.'' At the door he paused and turned. "Uh . . . Greta?''

"*Ja?*''

"When you check out, you might leave your phone number and address in Hamburg with the landlord. Who knows, I might come up with another villa soon.''

"*Ja!* I do that!''

"*Ja,* you do that.''

The car was an innocuous black Citroën. The driver was a stiff-upper-lip type whose only conversation was "Good evening, sir'' when Carter got in, and "Here we are, sir'' when the car stopped.

It was an MI6 safe house in the hills above San Roque. Carter was greeted at the door by another quiet type and escorted into a small study.

"Ah, here you are, Carter. Glad you were so prompt!"

"Thanks."

"Drink?"

"Whiskey, neat."

"Of course."

Sir Richard Witten-Jones was a tall, upright man with military shoulders and a long, lean English face. His shirt was custom made, and the light tan Savile Row suit was meticulously pressed. His English had a Welsh accent.

"There we are!"

Carter took the glass, returned the other man's salute, and drained half of it. They sat by a tall window facing the Mediterranean, and Witten-Jones launched right into it.

"I'm sure your chief told you most of it."

"The target, some of his background, and that it's a joint effort. I do the hit."

Witten-Jones made a slight face at Carter's American bluntness, but pulled it out with a smile.

"Our person on the inside is Miriam Lockwood. She has been Aflag's traveling companion for the last four months."

"As his mistress?"

"It would seem not. Evidently, he just likes to have a beautiful woman on his arm at all times. Other than that, he demands very little."

Witten-Jones passed Carter a five-by-seven head-and-shoulders photograph of a honey-blond woman who could have been staring at him from the cover of a fashion magazine.

"She's beautiful," he said, passing the photo back.

"You'll know her?"

"I'll know her." Carter nodded, lighting a cigarette and noting the agreement on Witten-Jones's face. He had looked at the photograph for five seconds. He had needed only three to memorize every feature in the girl's face.

"What color are her eyes?"

"Aquamarine," Carter said. "Dimple on the left cheek, tiny cleft in chin, slight mole under the right ear."

"Good enough," the Englishman said, a knowing smile curving his very proper mustache. "Aflag has been vacationing at a resort hotel in Marrakesh. This morning he drove into Tangier with Miriam and his two bodyguards. He told her that she should take only enough for two nights; it would be a short business trip. About an hour ago, she made contact. A big arms deal is being brokered somewhere in the mountains."

"Does she have it pinned down?"

"Hopefully yes, by now. If it is isolated enough, and the meeting is with, shall we say, disreputable people . . ."

"It's perfect for our situation."

"You'll leave right away. I'd like to fly you in by private plane, but that would make the authorities remember you."

"The night hydrofoil from Algeciras?"

"Yes. It leaves in an hour. That should give you ample time. Aflag is an inveterate gambler. He usually goes to the casino every night, wherever he is. I have already booked you into the Solizar. It is a tourist and businessman's hotel, large and very modern. No one on the staff will remember you."

"I've used it before."

"Good. If Miriam considers this meeting a go, you can get all the equipment you need from Emile St. Sharez. He is a wine merchant in Tangier."

Carter hooded his eyes and smoked as he took in the details of how to contact Emile St. Sharez through his daughter in Tangier.

"Can you give me an exact list of what you'll need?" Witten-Jones asked.

"It would be easier if I knew the locale."

"I realize that, but time may be a problem. Outline and overdo what you think you may need, and I'll pass it along."

Carter thought for a moment, trying to visualize every possible hang-up in his mind.

"I didn't bring any of my own tools, intentionally."

Witten-Jones nodded. "That was at my suggestion."

"Grenades, two flash and two M-80s. Can your boy get Russian hardware?"

"Easier than any other."

"Good. Make it an AK-47, but I want a Litton night scope that will fit it. Also, a Soviet 9mm Stechkin with a silencer."

"You wouldn't rather have a Laser sniper rifle?"

Carter shook his head. "It sounds like I'll need more firepower than accuracy."

"Good enough. Clothing?"

"Night gear . . . black heavy-knit turtleneck, black heavy-duty jeans, and durable boots. Throw in a Kevlar vest, too."

"Sizes?"

Carter rattled them off, then added, "And toss in a belt garrote, and a Fairbairon-Sykes with a sheath."

"It'll be taken care of."

Carter leaned forward and opened his eyes. "You didn't write anything down."

Witten-Jones grinned. "We've had the same training, my boy. My memory is every bit as good as yours."

An hour later, Carter was napping as the hydrofoil roared toward the port of Tangier.

The lifting of a well-shaped thigh over a barstool two spots down cleared Carter's vision.

Up close she was even more beautiful, but the makeup she now wore made her look much harder and much cheaper than her image in the picture.

"Champagne, please."

She hadn't bothered to do away with her English accent, but then there had probably been no need.

Carter smiled at her in the mirror. She cut him cold and sipped her champagne.

"Did we meet at Maxim's in Paris, or at Casa Botín in Madrid?"

"If we did, I'm sure I wouldn't remember."

"Are you on holiday?"

"No. Business."

"With your uncle?"

She laughed a low, husky laugh that didn't have an ounce of mirth in it. "Yes, with my uncle." She finished her drink.

"May I buy you another?" Carter asked, moving to the stool beside hers.

She shrugged. "Why not?"

Carter called the barman over and told him to bring two more drinks. She opened a small, sequined evening bag and took out a box of English cigarettes.

The barman beat Carter to the draw with his lighter.

"Is the gentleman bothering you, mademoiselle?" a voice asked.

He was about Carter's height, only about forty pounds heavier, and it didn't look like fat. He was calm, but Carter got the distinct impression that, if she gave the word, Carter's nose would be all over his face.

"Yes, but I'm rather enjoying it, Igor. Tell Hamir that I'll be over as soon as I finish my champagne and a little flirting."

One eye twitched, but the man turned and lumbered away.

"Igor?" Carter chuckled.

"Not really. His name is Rodesh. It amuses Hamir—my uncle—when I tease him about his muscle-bound boy-friend."

"You mean, he's . . . ?"

"Very light on his feet."

When she smiled, her face took on the same radiance as it had in the photograph.

"Do you suppose that, sometime tonight, you could slip away from your uncle and we could have a drink?"

"Sorry, when I'm locked in, I'm afraid it's for the night."

Her sultry eyes narrowed. Carter could tell that she was trying to tell him something, both with her eyes and the tone in her voice.

He couldn't get it.

"That's a pity. I guess I'll just have to go back to Spain celibate."

"Oh, dear, you needn't do that," she said with a laugh. "Sometimes he lets me have visitors! Excuse me now, I think I'll be leaving soon. I've suddenly got a splitting headache."

He watched all that marvelous movement under the dress as she moved across the room. Back at her station behind the old man, she leaned over and kissed him lightly on the cheek.

Carter cursed to himself under his breath and whirled back to face the bar.

Damn, he thought, a lot of double-talk, only half of which he had been able to decipher. She couldn't get out? Was it on or off? And if it was on, where and how in God's name was she going to brief him?

Then he saw the box of cigarettes she had left on the bar.

Carter darted a look at the group around the baccarat table. Aflag was currently holding the bank, so all his concentration was on the shoe and the cards. Igor, too, was looking at the table, but his expression was bored.

The lady looked tense, until Carter's hand snaked out, grabbed the box, and slid it into his jacket pocket.

"Another Chivas, *s'il vous plaît*."

"Of course, monsieur."

"The men's room?"

"Through the door and to the left, monsieur."

Carter navigated his way to the rest rooms, the box of cigarettes burning a hole in his pocket.

There were two gray-haired, corpulent gentlemen hailing from north of the Rhine standing at the urinals. Both were exclaiming in loud voices the cunning of thieving Arab croupiers.

Obviously the little Moroccan attendant didn't understand German, or else he just didn't give a damn. He stood behind them, brushing at their suits with a bland smile on his dark face.

The third stall was empty. Carter dived in, locked the door, dropped his pants, and sat. Gingerly he withdrew the cigarette box from his pocket and inspected it.

Nothing outside.

Carefully he pried the silver wrapper away from the inside of the box. It was there, a tightly folded note on onion skin:

I cannot get out once I'm in, unless I go with one of the bodyguards or Aflag. We are at the Acabar, east of the city, suites 8A, B, and C. I am in B. I sthere some way you can get to me? Send my cigarettes back via the barman. One of the two guards stays in the hall all the time. No one comes or goes without getting through them.

Carter turned the paper over and tried to imitate her small, precise English hand on the minuscule sheet she had provided: *At 1:00, sharp, tell your keeper you've ordered a snack from room service.*

He recreased the paper, slid it back into its space, and returned to the main gaming room.

At the bar, he held his impatience in check and sipped his drink. When he was sure that nothing had changed, he palmed the box of cigarettes and replaced them on the bar. He asked the barman for his bill.

"Oui, monsieur."

Seconds later, the barman presented the check. It was for 220 dirham. Carter placed a 500-dirham note on the tray, and only then seemed to notice the cigarettes.

"Ah, I believe that the lady—Monsieur Aflag's niece?—has forgotten her cigarettes."

"I will see that they are returned to her, monsieur."

"Merci. No change is needed."

"Merci beaucoup, monsieur."

The Killmaster was about to push open the casino's large glass front door and step into the street, when he saw the parked Mercedes limousine. If the opulence of the car didn't tell him who its owner was, the man leaning against the front fender, smoking, did.

He could have been Igor's twin.

It would never do, Carter thought, for both of them to recognize him so easily if he hoped to get into Miriam Lockwood's suite tonight with the ruse he hoped to use.

He backed away from the door and stared, casing the building for another way out. He started down the hall. There was a restaurant to the left, and directly ahead a set of spiral stairs that led down to a basement disco.

Guessing, he charged down the stairs. A doorman stood at the door leading into the disco, collecting a cover charge.

Carter took a one-hundred-dirham bill off his roll and folded it lengthwise so the zeros showed.

"I took a belly dancer to the casino. My wife is waiting outside the front door to kill me. Is there a way out from here? A back way?"

The man contemplated the note for an eternity before testily withdrawing it from the Killmaster's fingers and making it disappear in his cummberbund.

Carter remembered the barman upstairs.

Handy things, those cummerbunds.

"Wait . . . down there. I must get relief on the door."

Carter moved to the end of the hall and lounged. A minute later the man joined him, pulling a ring of keys from the bottomless cummerbund.

"In here."

Carter followed him into the men's room. He unlocked a small door flush in the tile wall, and led the Killmaster down a narrow passage and up a flight of stairs. At the top was a large storeroom.

"That door at the other end of the room is unlocked."

"You are a savior, *mon ami*!" Carter clapped the man on the shoulder and headed for the door.

Outside, three steps led up to a narrow alley. To the left was the Rue Marco Polo, to the right, the Rue Moliere.

His next stop was a nightclub, the Morocco Palace.

He turned right and, as he walked, kept darting glances over his shoulder. He still couldn't shake the feeling that, from somewhere in the shadows, he was being watched.

TWO

Her full name was Deleta St. Sharez, but just DELETA in bold red letters gleamed beneath her pictures in glass cases on either side of the nightclub's entrance.

Carter stepped just inside the door. A heavyweight with a fixed smile and a heavily scarred face bowed slightly from the waist.

"Good evening, monsieur. A table for one?"

"Is the show on now?"

"The second show is just ending, monsieur. Next show at two o'clock."

"Merci. I'll wait until that one."

Carter moved down the block, buying out flower vendors along the way. By the time he hit the alley that led back to the stage door, he looked like a moving hothouse.

"No one is allowed backstage, monsieur."

"Mademoiselle Deleta is expecting me."

"Merci, monsieur."

The secret of moving through Morocco was a pocketful of one-hundred-dirham notes.

Carter moved into the shadows of the wings and looked out at the lighted stage. From the rising crescendo of the music

15

and the constantly shifting light on the thrust stage, he could tell that her act was building to a close.

Then he saw her, all flesh and movement. She was short, with heavy hips, and her breasts were far too large for her height. Her skin was dark, her eyes large and brown, and her long hair pulled back behind her ears with silver combs was black as night.

She wore the traditional belly dancer's costume, and even where the gauzy material covered her body, it gave the illusion that she was naked.

Her feet were bare, and they moved her undulating body in time with the desert rhythms like a sensuous cat. Suddenly, the eerie wail of a flute joined the cymbals and drums. She became motionless, with her head thrown back and her breasts jutting, bulging above the spangled cups of her bra.

Her own voice wailed in perfect harmony with the flute as a gentle roll started in the muscles just beneath her breasts. Her hips joined in movement until the roll became a surging tide of flowing, rippling flesh.

Then, with a resounding thump of her pelvis and a final, keening wail, it was over and she was rushing toward the wings.

"Mademoiselle St. Sharez, with respects from Her Majesty's government and a simple man."

Carter thrust the flowers into her arms and, for the benefit of the doorman behind him, embraced her.

"You are . . . ?" she whispered in his ear.

"A man who is interested in fine old wines. I believe your father has a shipment for me."

"Your name?"

"Nick Carter."

"My dressing room is this way!"

Carter followed her across the backstage area, down a narrow, dimly lighted hallway, and into the room.

With the door closed and locked behind them, she dropped the mountain of flowers on the dressing table and turned to face him. In the more subdued lighting, her features were softer and her eyes became more alive.

They must make quite a pair, he thought, *this girl and her father*. She collected information every night in the club, and Emile passed it along, as well as other things.

"I have not seen my father since early this morning. I did not know you were coming over tonight."

Carter held up his hand. "The room?"

"Clean. Have you made contact?"

"Yes, at the casino. But she could say very little. I'm going out to the Acabar and will meet her in her suite at one."

"That will be difficult. Aflag has her watched nearly every minute of the day and night. I have only been able to reach her when she shops in the souk."

"I have a very simple way; it's usually the best. She spoke a lot of double-talk, but I think we're on. Where can I meet you?"

"I have one more show, at two."

"I know."

"Can you be back in the city by three?"

"It shouldn't be a problem," Carter said, and chuckled. "Unless I'm caught."

Her face lit up with a smile that took off even more years. "I like you, even though I don't like what you do. There is an all-night café just off the Grand Socco, near the entrance to the Medina. It is called Lamall."

"I can find it."

"I will meet you there at three."

"By the way, can you spare some makeup?"

"Some what?"

Carter was already at the dressing table. He selected some dark eyeliner and a dark pancake base. "Okay?"

"Sure," Deleta shrugged, amusement in her eyes. The sparkle quickly disappeared when he advanced on her with a pair of scissors. "What . . . what are you going to do?" she squeaked, backing away.

"Just borrowing a little of your hair, darling, from underneath. You'll never miss it. Our hair is very much the same color."

"But why?"

"You'll see. Do you have any spirit gum?"

"Yes, in the drawer—there. Sometimes I dance without a bra and I use it—"

Suddenly she realized that she had only met him five minutes before, and clamped her lips tightly shut.

"Pasties, I know," Carter said and grinned. "Ah, here we are."

Five minutes later he had fashioned a crude mustache by applying the dark hair to a shredded piece of nylon stocking with the glue.

"There," he said, pocketing the result and turning to her. "I'll see you at three, Allah willing."

Impulsively, he brushed her lips with his. Instead of smiling, a shudder ran through her body.

Well, Carter, he thought, *what the hell did you expect? She knows what you're here for.*

He pressed another bill into the watchman's hand on the way out. "A thousand thanks."

"Merci, monsieur, merci."

Carter emerged into the darkness of the alley and turned left toward a curve that would take him back out on Boulevard Mohammed V and easy access to a taxi.

He was just around the curve, with the lights of the boulevard winking dimly eighty yards ahead, when a tall, bulky figure stepped from a rear service doorway.

"Hello, Carter. How's it goin'?"

The Killmaster froze, his body at once rigidly alert, his right forearm tensing as if Hugo's sheath, with its spring release that would send the deadly stiletto into the palm of his right hand, were still there.

But it wasn't.

And his 9mm Luger, Wilhelmina, was not in its usual shoulder rig under his left armpit.

He hadn't brought his tools this time, and as he strained his eyes toward the dark figure, he felt totally naked.

A lighter flared and came up to the tip of a cigarette.

"Hello, Edell."

Jake "The Hammer" Edell, renegade ex-CIA operative, Near East and Africa. They called him "The Hammer" because of his brutality. He rarely needed a weapon. Carter himself had seen the man pound many another human being into pulp with just the sides of his rock-hard fists.

Edell had been run out of the Company about three years before, for everything from padding his expense account to suspicion of selling out his own comrades for profit. In fact, the man would seel anybody or anything for profit. He was a very rotten apple in an otherwise generally clean barrel.

About a year before, he had been indicted for hijacking a shipment of U.S. arms and diverting them to a rebel band in Central America. That had driven him undercover.

"I thought maybe someone would have nailed you by now, Edell."

"No way. Too mean to die, you know that."

"Yeah, I do."

Now Carter knew why he had sensed a tail all night but hadn't spotted it. Edell was good, well trained. Maybe as good as the Killmaster himself.

"I've been working Algeria and Morocco. Odd jobs . . . guns, a little information. Whatever I can pick up."

"And Libya?"

The massive shoulders shrugged in outline against the boulevard's lights. "Everybody's money spends."

His shifting position had brought his right arm into silhouette. It hung loosely at his side, palm to the rear.

Carter knew there was a finely balanced stiletto, much like his own, under the sleeve of Edell's shirt. He also knew that the loosely hanging arm could come up like a cobra striking and send the blade into a pinpoint target at twice the distance that now separated them.

"I'm going to light a cigarette, Edell."

"Go ahead."

Carefully, Carter extracted a cigarette and lighter. As he went through the ritual, his mind raced. Surely Edell knew Aflag, at least by sight. He probably knew and/or dealt with half the scum from Cairo to Rabat. Had there been a leak? Had Aflag sent Edell blind, just for insurance?

"I meet the hydrofoil every night. Sometimes I get care packages from Barcelona or Madrid. When I spotted you tonight, I just tagged along. See, I remember you, Nick. You rarely go anywhere without something going down."

"Not this time," Carter said, suppressing a sigh of relief. "Just a vacation."

The laugh was low, guttural, and menacingly without humor. "Bullshit. I saw you playing chitchat with Aflag's broad in the casino. You checked into the Solizar with only a small bag. You and I both know that means you're moving fast. Now you're connecting with Deleta St. Sharez. I don't know her whole scam yet, but I know she's connected."

"All coincidence."

"I wonder if Hamir Aflag would think so."

"Just trying to score on a boring evening, Edell."

"Don't shit one who knows, Carter. Aflag's big with the boys in red lately. That makes him prime for wet stuff."

"What do you want, Edell?"

"What I always want—a little spending money. What's it worth if I forget that you're in Tangier and go south for a few days rest?"

There it was, clear, cut, and dried. Carter would have to kill him.

"You've got me," Carter growled, moving toward him. "I've only got expenses on me in cash."

"You can get more."

The Killmaster was four paces from him when he flipped the cigarette full in the man's face. He followed it with his body, a shoulder hard in the gut.

Edell landed well, rolled, and came up in a crouch, with

the stiletto in his left hand and a blackjack in his right.

Carter guessed that the man would only kill him as a last resort. Dead, Carter couldn't pay. And, thankfully, that was all Edell wanted.

"Dumb, Carter . . . damned stupid," Edell hissed.

"Hand-to-hand, I can kill you, Edell, and you know it."

"Maybe, but I got these. And if you were carrying, you'd have something out by now."

The blackjack made a whooshing sound through the air, and Carter saw the stiletto come up from his other side.

Stopping the blade was the wiser of two possible moves.

He caught Edell's wrist with one hand and locked the elbow with the other. At the same time, he turned his side into the other man's body and took the brunt of the sap's power in the middle of his back, high between his shoulder blades.

The pain from the blow was hell, but not one-tenth of the pain he planned to inflict.

Carter turned the arm over and brought it down with all the power he could over his rising knee.

Edell was good. He saw the intent, and moved his front close to Carter's rear. It worked. Instead of snapping the forearm like a twig, all the Killmaster could do was give him a bad bruise.

At the same time, Edell used his superior body weight to force Carter into the wall. He managed to get his head to the side, but not his shoulder.

Bolts of pain shot down his arm to tingle the tips of his fingers, as well as a deadening sensation that crept halfway to the small of his back.

"Got you, you bastard!"

"Like hell," Carter said, driving his elbow into the man's gut and jamming a heel into his instep at the same time.

Carter was free and retreating down the alley to regroup. But Edell was right behind him. The man was not only a street fighter, but he was also a trained one, and he was impervious to pain. It was also obvious that he had kept himself in perfect condition. That, coupled with the fact that he had forty pounds on Carter, told the Killmaster not to get in close with him again.

Carter was almost to the stage door of the nightclub, when he whirled in a crouch, ready to go again.

Edell was coming in fast and low, both arms swinging wide and forward. Again the sap caught Carter, this time in the ribs, only to be followed by the stiletto cleaving his jacket from armpit to tail.

"Gonna hammer you, Carter . . . gonna hammer you and then cut you."

There wasn't much doubt about it now: rage had replaced reason. Carter could tell that from the random way the stiletto was cutting swaths of air closer and closer to his chest.

He backpedaled and again hit stucco, but this time on two sides. He was in a corner. Edell crouched even lower and came in for the kill.

Carter dodged a swing from each weapon and poised for a desperation dive, when light suddenly flooded the alley and both their suspended forms from a door on the right.

A young Moroccan boy, his dark face shades lighter than normal, stood in the light, gaping at the knife in Edell's hand. A frightened curse left his lips in a combination of both Arabic and French. He dropped the garbage bags he held, and took off down the alley as if he were pursued by the hounds of hell.

Edell had turned partially to the light. Before he tried to spin back, Carter dived, catching his right arm just at the elbow, snaping the wrist over as hard as he could.

The stiletto clattered to the stones at their feet. Both men dived for it, Edell swinging the blackjack as he moved.

The Killmaster won and, in the same motion, rolled into the other man's twisting body, further unbalancing him. The sap hit the stones on the far side of Carter's body, with the other man's fingers under it.

He howled in pain, released the sap, and tried to roll away.

Carter rolled with him and came up on top, straddling his chest. A handful of hair and a quick yank brought the man's face a foot from Carter's and his throat an inch from the blade.

"You're dead, Edell."

"Fuck you!" He tried to buck Carter off.

But he only tried once.

The AXE agent lunged. The point of the blade went in through the man's right nostril. The body twitched for a full five seconds with four inches of steel in its brain.

And then it was still, lifeless, the eyes wide in shocked death.

Carter rolled away to his knees and caught his breath as he quickly went through alternatives. Edell was obviously known to all the lowlifes in North Africa. With Aflag in Tangier, and something big obviously going down, police informants would surely put out the word.

Also, there was the fact that the boy had spotted them. He might have caught enough of their faces to pinpoint Carter.

"Dammit," he hissed aloud, "what lousy luck."

He made the only decision he could. Edell's body would have to disappear, at least until the operation was over . . . and, hopefully, forever.

Hoisting the dead weight into a fireman's carry over his shoulder, he sprinted back to the curve in the alley. With one hand he lifted the lid of a huge garbage dumpster and heaved the body inside.

It couldn't stay there, but it was a place to park it until he could make other arrangements.

Back at the stage door, he did the best he could to rearrange himself, and went boldly inside.

"Forgot to tell Mademoiselle St. Sharez something," he mumbled.

The old man hardly looked up from his newspaper.

Carter was becoming part of the backstage family.

He didn't take time to knock.

He should have.

Deleta was standing in the middle of the room, with two older, djellaba-clad women bustling around her. From the look of things, they were her dressers and they had just started.

She was covered from her navel down by a new gauzy skirt, but that was as far as the dressers had gotten.

"What is it?" She spoke without making any attempt to cover the heavy, conical breasts that jutted with insolence from her body.

"Problems."

"Serious?"

"I think so . . . very."

She snapped her fingers as a command. The women gave up trying to cover their mistress's nudity and headed toward the door. They gave Carter appraising glances in passing.

"What has happened?"

"A man tried to shake me down just now in the alley. His name is Edell, ex-American CIA."

" 'Ex' . . . ?"

"A renegade. He's wanted in several countries. I didn't know he was in North Africa, or even alive."

"Does he suspect?" she gasped, her beautiful dark eyes widening to saucer size.

"No, I'm sure of it. He was only looking for a payday to keep his mouth shut about me being in Tangier."

Her shoulders dropped in relief. "Did you pay him?"

"No, I killed him. I put the point of his own stiletto in his brain. That's the problem . . . the body."

Deleta suddenly looked a little sick and turned away.

Carter lit a cigarette to give her time to adjust. It was about the way he figured. Deleta was good only so far. When it came to wet work—and it got close to her—she had to adjust.

She moved haltingly, pulling on a robe at last, to the bench before the dressing table. She didn't bother to belt the robe, so both breasts were still bare to the ruddy brown of their nipples. Through cigarette smoke, Carter watched those nipples rise and fall as the woman got back her breath.

When they steadied, he spoke again. "The body is in the garbage dumpster. I don't think it's a good place to leave it. It's almost twelve now. I meet Miriam at one."

"You want me to arrange a . . . a disposal."

"A nice lonesome desert burial, if possible."

He waited several seconds for an answer, and when none came he spoke again, putting an extra harshness in his voice.

"Can you do it, Deleta?"

"Yes. I can arrange to have it done."

She stood and turned to face him. Close against him, she was tiny. He looked straight down into her upturned face. The determination he saw there erased the doubts he had been entertaining.

"And *will* you do it?"

"I will."

Carter turned on his heel and, without another word, left the room.

On Boulevard Mohammed V, he grabbed a taxi.

"You know the resort, Acabar?"

"Oui, monsieur."

"How long?"

"Forty, forty-five minutes."

Carter held a wad of bills under the driver's nose. "Can you make it in less time, with one quick stop at the Solizar?"

"Thirty minutes. Get in!"

Carter took less than five minutes at the Solizar to grab his empty bag and return to the cab.

THREE

The Acabar was a twin-towered monster facing the ocean about three miles to the east of the city. The lobby was in the middle, facing an outdoor restaurant and an Olympic-sized pool.

"Want to make the same fare in about an hour and a half back to the city?" Carter asked the taxi driver.

"*Mais oui, monsieur!*"

"Meet me down there . . . at the highway."

The man was all smiles as Carter entered the lobby. If this big American was going to rob the Acabar and he needed a ride back to the city afterward, that was all right.

The Arabs were wonderful that way, thought Carter. Live and let live.

Halfway across the lobby, Carter figured out from the mailboxes that even numbers were on the left, odd in the tower to the right.

"I don't have a reservation."

"We have space, sir. Your passport?"

Carter handed it over, then glanced up at the pseudoantique clock. It was 12:35.

"Suite or room, sir?"

"Your suites are all on the top two floors, right?"

"Yes, sir."

"Give me one on the tenth floor, please."

"Of course. Suite Eleven."

"Uh, do you have one in the other building? I like to wake up and look at the mountains."

"Most assuredly. Suite Fourteen."

"Thank you."

The elevator stopped at the tenth floor, and Carter followed the bellman through a lot of marble to the suite. He carried his own bag.

"Breakables," he had said.

The bellman only shrugged. He got a tip just for being a guide through the building's maze of corridors. Three doors down from his suite, Carter spotted the chute opening down to the incinerator.

"Is everything all right, sir?"

"Fine," Carter replied, pressing a hundred into the man's hand and seeing him to the door.

It had barely closed before the Killmaster was on the phone.

"Room service, please."

"*Oui, monsieur.*"

Click, click. Buzz, buzz.

"Good evening—room service."

"I would like a plate of sandwiches, some cheeses, a large bottle of Perrier, and two boxes of Rothman cigarettes."

"*Oui, monsieur.*"

"I'd like that as soon as possible. There's a hundred dirhams for you if I can have it immediately."

"*Oui, oui, monsieur.*"

Carter threw off his coat and went to work with the makeup. It wouldn't have to be a perfect job, just enough to darken his skin and hollow his eyes. He also did a quick restyle of his hair, parting it in the middle and combing it down over his ears.

By the time the knock came on the door, it was complete save for the mustache.

"Room service."

"*Oui*." He let the white-jacketed waiter into the room. "Over there, on the coffee table."

"*Oui, monsieur*."

He moved across the room with Carter in step right behind him, gauging his size.

The fit would be a little snug, Carter guessed, but thieves couldn't always be choosers.

The waiter set the tray down and turned just as Carter's two hands grasped the side of his neck. Deftly, the Killmaster's thumbs found the pressure points just behind the ears, and squeezed.

The waiter went down and out without making a sound.

The jacket was a little tight, but by leaving the top three buttons open, it didn't look too bad. The black bow tie was a clip-on, and the cummerbund fit perfectly without adjustment. The last step was the mustache over his upper lip.

It was 1:05.

Tray in hand, Carter took the elevator to the next floor down. It was pretty easy to spot the three suites. Igor's twin lolled, reading in a lounge chair against the opposite wall. Like his boyfriend, he was trim in every way, with a short haircut and a dark, expensive three-piece suit complete with bulge under the left armpit.

He seemed engrossed in the magazine, but Carter could sense as he moved forward that the man's vigilance was ten on a ten-to-one scale.

The Killmaster shrunk his height as much as possible and hunkered his head far into the white jacket as he rang the bell beside the door marked 8-B.

Out of the corner of his eye, he saw the man unwrap

himself from the lounge and head his way.

"Yes?"

"Room service for Mademoiselle Lockwood."

The door opened just as Igor II lifted the lid on one of the tray's dishes and purloined a sandwich.

Carter hoped the relief didn't show on the side of his face.

"Take it into the bedroom."

Carter was sure he heard a growling laugh from the man in the hall before Miriam closed the door in his face.

He set the tray on a wide, circular table at the foot of the bed, and turned to face her.

"How . . . ?"

"The waiter's sleeping peacefully upstairs in my suite."

"They told me you were good," she said with a shake of her head. "Over here."

Carter followed her to her vanity and watched as she pawed behind the mirror.

Since returning to the hotel, she had scrubbed her face. A lot of hard years had come off with the makeup. Her long, honey-blond hair was pulled back from her face now. The style accentuated her high cheekbones and added to the slant of her eyes. The unusually light cast to her skin gave a Madonna-like aura to her features.

But Carter knew she was anything but a Madonna. Her prominently displayed body in a sheer negligee proved that.

"Something wrong?" she asked, noting his look.

"Not a thing," Carter said, grinning. "Pardon me for staring, but I can see why Aflag posts a guard out there."

Miriam chuckled sardonically. "He just wants something pretty and feminine on his arm for the social scene. He gets his kicks with . . ." She paused and glanced toward the door.

"Igor and his clone?"

"Yes," she said, and accompanied it with a laugh that washed all tension away between them.

She was extracting two pieces of onion skin from the

envelope she had taken from behind the mirror. Carefully, she flattened them on the vanity.

"Do you know the area on the Med side of Morocco, from Ceuta in the north down to Tetuan?"

"Not well."

"Highway 28 runs it north and south. I have made a crude map from the highway cutoff out to the bay at Cabo Negro."

"Good girl."

"Much of the seacoast . . . here, and here . . . has been built up with resort complexes."

Carter chuckled. "Club Med is everywhere."

"Exactly. But there are private areas, here along the Cabo Negro cliffs, that are totally secluded. As I say, the map is crude, but I have tried to give you distances and topography to Aflag's villa."

"He owns it?"

"Not in his own name. He leases it through a holding company he owns blind in the Canary Islands. A small bank in Zürich owns the villa."

"And Aflag owns the bank."

She nodded. "Under another blind holding company. A great deal of his business is transacted here, but he never stays there more than a day and a night, two at the most."

"You've been there?"

"Only once, but I managed to get around the grounds and cover most of the villa."

Carter followed her fingers as they moved to the second piece of onion skin. "This is the interior?"

"Yes. It's three floors, and as you can see, it's spread over quite an area. It's built right on the side of the cliff, sheer, unscalable. The grounds are protected by an electrified fence."

"Dogs?"

"Not when I was there the last time, but roving guards day and night."

"How many?"

"Four, when I was there."

"How far from the nearest populated area?"

"About three miles. Noise would be no problem."

Carter leaned closer to the maps. They were roughly sketched but they included a great amount of detail. He had little doubt that he could work from them.

He was about to ask her a few more questions, when Miriam suddenly spun him around and glued her body to his. All in one motion, she pulled his hands around her body until they held her firm buttocks and covered his lips with hers.

A sultry moan emanated from her throat as she writhed against him. He could feel all of her move at the same time . . . her breasts, her pelvis, and her muscular thighs.

For a brief instant he recoiled, but quickly joined in. He was pretty sure Miriam Lockwood wasn't wildly seducing him in some mad, nymphomaniacal urge.

And then he saw it: a shadow move in the crack of the partially opened door.

"The bed!" she gasped, pushing Carter backward with the heat of her body. "I can wait no longer. Hurry!"

He obliged, letting her push him down across the bed. She stood above him like a blond-haired pagan goddess, doing a shimmy with her shoulders and hips. The gown she wore took on a life of its own, sliding down her body, imitating the unveiling of a statue.

She was magnificent. She stood before him, her hands on her hips, letting him survey her. His breath caught in his throat as he gazed at her superb body. Her breasts were full and heavy, but they had no trace of droop about them; they stood forward, high firm globes, maintaining their roundness even in nudity. Below them, her body tapered leanly, then broadened suddenly at the hips. Her thighs were muscled like an athlete and her buttocks were curved and dimpled without a hint of flabbiness.

Carter looked at her, feeling a chocking sensation at the

sheer loveliness before him. He closed his eyes for an instant, then opened them quickly. She was still there, solid and real.

She held out her hands to him.

"Hurry," she breathed. "Please . . . I need you."

Suddenly she was over him, his face pressed into the scented softness between her breasts. Like a serpent she slid down until, once again, her lips locked over his.

It was all Carter could do in the stillness of the room to keep the fact in his mind that this was an act.

Then they both heard it, the gentle click of the door.

Miriam turned the ardor off like a faucet, jumped from the bed, and padded to the door. In seconds she was back, nonchalantly pulling the gown up over her glorious nudity.

"The bastards," she hissed. "They get their kicks that way."

Carter checked his mustache and straightened his tie. "Won't they tell Aflag?"

"Of course," she said with a smile, moving back to the vanity and the maps. "He expects me to have little flings now and then, since he's not interested that way."

Carter was tempted to ask her how many little "flings" she had had in the last few months, all in the line of duty, of course. But it was none of his business how she did her job, and she was already back and seated beside him on the bed.

"What else do you need to know?"

"Chain of events, mainly."

"Of course, sorry." She accepted a cigarette and a light. "We leave tomorrow around nine, and arrive at the villa about noon."

"Which bedroom is yours?" Carter asked, pointing to the sketch of the villa's interior.

"Here. The study is here. That's where Aflag always meets with his business associates. They'll all arrive in the afternoon, by car. I won't see them. They bring dinner up to my room."

"When will they be all together?"

"At dinner, of course. After the meal, Aflag usually naps for a couple of hours. Then they usually sit down around eleven or midnight to talk, and it could go on all night."

"How many servants?"

"Only one, a cook. Rodesh and Aleve do the serving."

"Aleve is Igor Two?"

"Yes," she chuckled.

"All right—one cook, two inside bodyguards, and four outside watchdogs. How many guests?"

"That I can't say, for sure. But I don't think more than three. I managed to overhear a few phone calls from Marrakesh. Arms are involved in this trip, but there's something more important."

"Like what?"

Miriam shrugged. "I don't know. But whoever Aflag's meeting is going to pay Red Star with some service rather than money."

"Red Star? Moscow?"

"It would figure. Or it could be Aflag's KGB control."

"See if you can find out more on the ride up tomorrow," Carter said, and stood to leave. "I'll be coming in about the dinner hour. Everyone should be busiest then."

"Wait . . . you can't go yet."

"Why not?"

She twisted his wrist around until she could see the face of his watch. "We wouldn't have finished yet. Drink?"

"Why not?" Carter chuckled. "If we can't dance."

The look Miriam gave him didn't say yes for later, but it didn't say no, either.

They killed another twenty minutes over scotch and questions from Carter to refine the topography around the villa.

Then Miriam ushered him to the door. She opened it with a flourish and moved into his arms. The seduction act was only toned down a few degrees, and finally she released him.

"Tip him, Aleve."

Carter found himself in the hall, and the door slammed behind him. Igor II shoved some bills in his jacket pocket and nodded toward the elevator with a look of disgust on his face.

Carter shuffled as humbly as possible to the elevator, and sweated until the door opened. He pushed "8" and waited. When the door opened again, he darted into the hall and found the stairs.

Back on the tenth floor, he entered his own suite and immediately checked the waiter. The man was sleeping peacefully.

Carter stripped his pockets and put the contents in his bag. He then went through the suite, stuffing linens and anything else of value into the bag. This done, he removed the makeup and replaced the waiter's jacket, tie, and cummerbund.

In the hall, he pushed the bag down the incinerator chute and made for the stairs. On the ground floor, he stayed in rear hallways until he found the kitchen exit.

He had to wait another fifteen minutes for a pair of dishwashers to take a break, but when the coast was clear he darted through the exit and ran.

In no time he skirted the perimeter of the hotel and vaulted a low stone fence.

The taxi was waiting.

"Tangier, monsieur?"

"*Oui*," Carter replied, and gave him an address three blocks from the Grand Socco. At the same time, he dropped another wad of bills into the man's hand.

Leaning back in the seat, he contemplated the lights of Tangier through the cab's windshield and started to plan the hit and the escape.

Carter left a much richer and very happy cabdriver, and dawdled on the street corner until the taxi was gone toward the center of the new town. When he was sure that no one on the street was paying him any attention, he strolled in the direction of the huge square that fronted the Casbah and Medina, the Grand Socco.

This time of the morning, the huge open area was nearly deserted. There were a few early-morning soup sellers, pushcart vendors, and an occasional beggar, but none of them gave him a second glance.

The café was easy to find. All he had to do was check the narrow alleys off the square. The Lamall was in the third one, about a hundred yards down.

Inside was a dimly lit haze, more like a Chinese opium den than a Moroccan coffeehouse. The men were dressed in a hodgepodge of Western and native Moroccan dress. The women were all in traditional djellabas, both stark white and black, with a double veil around their heads and over their faces.

The men occupied tables in the center of the room. The women were segregated to wooden benches attached to the walls.

Carter took a small table near the door that gave him a view of the street as well as all of the interior. He ordered mint tea and a *kab el ghzal*. When it came, he relished the tea, but could barely finish the ultrasweet pastry stuffed with almond paste.

His eyes scanned the women on the benches. With only eyes staring from the veils' narrow openings, and even the forehead covered, it was impossible to tell ages. He went by height and what he could discern of weight, and canceled out all but three of them.

By alternating his gaze at each one of these, he was able to spot Deleta's occasional glances at him. She sat demurely, a woven straw shopping bag on her lap with two loaves of bread sticking out the top.

Now and then she answered a comment from a woman nearby, but mostly she sipped her mint tea and made sure

Carter had spotted her. Twice she placed money on the table before her, only to snatch it back with a look at him.

Finally, Carter got the picture. He dropped a bill on his own table and exited into the street. Just short of the square he stopped, lit a cigarette, and inspected the clear night sky.

He heard the soft tap of her footsteps behind him and didn't even look down as she brushed past.

"Follow me!"

He did, at about twenty paces through the tall, arched gate into the Medina. They were barely through the gate when she veered off the main street into one that was barely two men wide.

Carter followed, and practically crashed into her in the darkness.

"Here, put this on!"

She handed him a tentlike, long-sleeved djellaba with a hood.

"What happened to Edell?"

"Two of my father's people took his body to the sea. He will go out with the morning fishermen. My father is very angry."

"I don't blame him, but it was just a sorry coincidence."

"Let us hope so. Men like him usually have friends."

Carter had just finished adjusting the hood over his head when a short dark man in Western dress appeared in a pool of light in the main street they had just left.

"Be calm," Deleta whispered. "It is Ahmed. He will make sure we are not followed."

"I take it we're not going to your father's wine shop?"

"No. We go to the place where he conducts his other business and stores the type of supplies used by people like you."

He didn't comment on her sarcastic tone of voice, and followed her without question along the incredibly narrow, winding streets. There were no lights, and they heard only the occasional sound of a baby's wail or the sudden bark of a dog as they walked past the tightly shuttered stuccoed buildings.

All of the streets in this medieval part of the city were as they had been for hundreds of years, hardly more than alleys, sided by crumbling whitewashed walls with no break.

Now and then a sleeping beggar appeared in a doorway, or they would have to make way for a vendor on his way for an early start in the Socco. Other than that, they saw no one.

As they moved into the very center of the Medina, Deleta stepped up her pace, suddenly disappearing around a corner. Carter had to move quickly, keeping track of her more by sense than sight. He knew from past experience that a Westerner in this labyrinth of alleyways could be lost for hours.

His eyes bored through the darkness until he spotted her. A hand came from the depths of her tentlike robe and motioned him to join her.

"Where?"

"Here," she said, and produced a key. The heavy, inlaid door swung open and she literally danced inside, motioning him to follow.

Carter stepped into a vaulted foyer and flattened his back against the dark paneling.

"Come!"

She was already moving from the alcove down a long, white-stuccoed hallway. Carter followed, his eyes darting right and left through low, indented archways leading to darkened rooms no larger than a medieval monk's cell.

The hallway widened to reveal a tiny indoor garden with a small round fountain in its center. Across the garden, they came to a wooden stairwell. At the top, a huge native, dressed like Carter, stepped from the shadows.

Deleta barked something, and the man melted back into the darkness. A door groaned open and a figure appeared in the dim illumination.

"Deleta?"

"Yes, Father."

She brushed past him into the room, and Carter followed. The door was closed and an oil lamp turned up.

"Monsieur Carter?"

"Yes."

"I am Emile St. Sharez."

The man was tall and reed thin, with salt and pepper hair. His eyes were slightly watery and deep brown behind half-glasses that rested on his very Gallic nose.

"Monsieur St. Sharez," Carter said, shaking the man's proffered hand, "I cannot thank you enough."

A shrug. "There is no need for thanks. I am very well paid for what I do, and I happen to believe in what you are about to do. Though I must admit I am worried about your adventure earlier this evening."

"As I told Deleta, I am sure it was just a coincidence." Carter went on to explain Edell in detail. By the time he was finished, the Frenchman seemed placated.

"Very well. Some things cannot be avoided, I suppose. But now down to the business at hand. You saw the woman, Lockwood?"

"I did."

Carter produced the two sheets of onion skin and went over everything Miriam Lockwood had told him. Then he added his own thoughts.

"I would like to leave yet tonight, if possible. If you could supply me with a car and a driver, I could sleep during the trip and do my reconnoitering just after dawn."

"I have already thought of that."

St. Sharez moved to the door and called softly. Seconds later, the man Carter had seen earlier stepped into the room. In the light, he was even larger. He was at least six feet tall, and his skin was a copper color. He stood straight and proud.

"Monsieur Carter, Yashif Beirmaudi. He will be your

guide, your driver, and can give you any other assistance you may need. He will also give you his life, if necessary. He is a Tuareg, one of the 'blue people.' ''

Carter nodded; nothing else needed to be said. The Killmaster knew that before him stood one of the bravest and fiercest fighters in the world.

"Do you have a map of eastern Morocco?"

"Of course." He produced one and spread it out on the table.

Carter studied it for a full ten minutes, and then made his decision.

"Once the operation is over, the woman and I will be able to hopefully escape by car. But only a certain amount of distance can be traveled safely on the roads. It would be equally dangerous to travel back over the Rif to Tangier, or down to Casablanca."

"Then what do you propose?"

"M'diq, here, is a short distance from Cabo Negro. Yashif, you are familiar with it?"

"I know it well," the Tuareg giant nodded. "It is a small fishing village. There is a resort and a few villas owned by foreigners, but they pay little attention to the natives."

"Do you know any of the fishermen?"

"All of them."

"If we could get away from M'diq by fishing boat and sail here, close to Ceuta, we could go overboard and be in the Spanish territory by dawn."

"Excellent," St. Sharez said. "A brilliant plan. They will be checking all the roads and the frontiers, and you will already be on Spanish soil."

"That's right," Carter said, thankful that Spain, when she had given up her share of Morocco as a colony, had had the good sense to retain the tiny tip of Ceuta on the Moroccan side of the Strait of Gibraltar as a military base.

"I can make the arrangements," Yashif declared.

"Good. Now the equipment."

"This way," St. Sharez said, leading them into an adjoining room.

He lifted the lid of a huge rattan trunk, and stepped back.

It took Carter less than ten minutes to see that not only was it all there, but it was also new and in excellent working order.

"Satisfied?"

"More than satisfied," he replied. "How soon can we leave?"

"As soon as my people have loaded the car."

FOUR

The afternoon was quickly fading into twilight, the air becoming cool and slightly damp. The sky above was a weak blue now and, behind Carter, turning slightly red where the sun dipped over the Rif Mountains.

The Killmaster was wedged into a craggy nook on the cliffs above the sea. To his left, perched on a lower cliff, he had a clear view of Hamir Aflag's house and grounds.

The arms dealer had chosen the spot well. It sat on the very edge of a hundred-foot sheer cliff. Even one man scaling it would have sounded like an army.

No entrance from the sea.

The house itself was vast, with two-story white stucco walls, windows shaded by colorful awnings, elaborate balconies at two sides, and towering trees around it. A garden of red, blue, and yellow flowers covered the area between the house and the road where there was an iron-grilled gate with brick posts at either side. A graveled drive led from the gate to the house. The entire estate was surrounded by a brick fence topped with iron spikes.

Even an amateur would have spotted the wiring running

along the top of the wall and seen that the spikes were electrified.

Carter had done a recon early that morning before dawn and had mapped out a plan. Since then, he and Yashif Beirmaudi had spelled each other watching the comings and goings around the villa and timing the guards.

Aflag, Miriam, and the two Igors had arrived just after noon. About three, the guests had started showing up, four of them, all in separate cars.

And quite a guest list it was.

Carter had recognized high-ranking representatives from German, Italian, and IRA terrorist groups. The fourth man was familiar, but Carter couldn't put a tag on him.

With this kind of company, he was pretty sure that Miriam's guess was right. Aflag was helping to set up something far more important than an ordinary arms deal.

But that was neither here nor there. The target was Hamir Aflag. If a few bullyboys got bagged along with the big man, so much the better.

He didn't bother to turn at the sound of boots scraping against stone behind him. He had become accustomed to Yashif's tread.

An hour before, the Tuareg had taken the car and driven to the village of M'diq. From the look on his face, the trip had been successful.

"There is no problem," the man declared, setting a large paper bag between them. "His name is Karem. He wants to know nothing, and he will remember nothing. He has already been paid. His boat is not fast, but it is seaworthy."

"Good," Carter said, handing over the binoculars. "I'm going down to change."

Darkness was gathering fast as the Killmaster made his way down the inland side of the rocky cliff. The big rattan basket was cached at its base in a stand of scrub trees.

He stripped and pulled on the dark clothing. Over the turtleneck, he fastened the Kevlar vest. It was specially rigged with harness and snaps for the grenades and extra magazines for the silenced Stechkin and the AK-47. The piano-wire garrote was built into the belt of the vest, and also held a holster for the Stechkin and the sheath containing the deadly Fairbairon-Sykes commando knife.

At the last minute, he had requested and got a second Stechkin to pass on to Miriam. This he anchored to his right ankle under the top of his boot.

He checked everything a second time and, palming a tin of blackout grease, climbed back up to join Yashif.

"Anything new?"

"Lights coming on. Quite a bit of movement inside. The woman came out on the terrace a little while ago, top floor on the corner there, seaside."

Carter nodded. "That's her suite. The guards?"

"Same schedule. Three patrolling while one takes a two-hour break."

Carter shifted around until he got comfortable. Yashif did the same, and opened the sack he had brought. From it he took the clips, the wiring, and the nylon line that Carter had requested, also some sandwiches. He passed two of them to Carter. From under his shirt he produced a bottle of wine.

"You drink wine?" Carter commented.

"I am a good Moslem on holy days," Yashif chuckled, applying a corkscrew to the bottle. "You will kill them all?"

"If I can."

"It is a nasty business."

"Yes, it is."

A chilling laugh rolled from the big Moroccan's barrel chest as he raised the bottle. "To success!"

Carter belly-crawled the last hundred yards to the power relay box, even though he knew he probably couldn't be seen from the house. Earlier that afternoon, with the binoculars, he had traced the feeder line from the villa out to the box. It looked to be the relay for all three of the isolated villas in the area.

The short tower was steel, with built-in climbing pegs. It took only seconds to reach the box and pick the padlock that protected it.

With a penlight, he went over the wires. They were color-coded, but he could tell from the direction which wires went to which villa.

Carefully he rigged a large alligator clip to the input feed, and then grounded it to the box. Then he marked the overload cutoff with tape and attached a second wire to the hot input, leaving its end dangling.

By the time he reached the bottom of the pole, Yashif was waiting.

"You sure you've got it?"

"Positive," the man replied. "I give you five minutes to get in place, then kill the power for thirty seconds."

"Right. Up you go!"

Carter, the AK-47 slung over his back, darted along the edge of the cliff toward the compound. He was only partially shielded by trees, but there was no break in the wall on this side for observing, and from the house, only someone on the third floor or roof could see him.

No one had ventured on the roof all day, and the third floor on this side of the villa was dark.

As he jogged, he uncoiled the nylon line from around his waist and shook out a lariat. In just under three minutes he was under the wall, gently swinging the loop in his right hand.

There was only a sliver of pale moon illuminating the sky. Against it he picked out a pair of the iron spikes atop the wall and got ready. His only indication of the power outage would be a subtle shift in shadows far to his right against the cliff descending to the front of the villa.

When he guessed fifteen seconds to go, he started gently rolling the loop around his head.

It came, a barely perceptible darkening of the cliff face and the narrow winding road.

Carter lofted the lariat's loop, held his breath as it soared, then sighed with relief when it settled over the iron spikes.

He brought the line taut and applied the rubber soles of his boots to the wall. Hand over hand, as silent as a cat, he climbed.

If the guards had kept to their measured rounds, this immediate area of the garden would be deserted.

At the top he dropped the line and pulled himself the last few feet by the spikes themselves.

Quickly, he checked the area.

Empty.

He unfastened the line, coiled it, and dropped into the garden running. Ten seconds later he was at the side of the house and making his way toward the rear in darkness.

By the time the lights blazed again, Carter was already scaling the wall, using a drainpipe and heavy bougainvillaea vines in his ascent. Several times he selected a vine too small to support his weight and slipped back.

When this happened, he hung precariously for several seconds to make sure the sound of his thrashing body hadn't been detected.

At last he reached the edge, hoisted himself over, and dropped to the roof. It was graveled, noisy. He removed his boots and, as quietly as possible, ran the length of the villa to the other wing.

Miriam's suite was in the rear corner, with windows and balconies on both sides. He chose the rear side, which would be the sitting room, and looped the line over an air-conditioning vent.

The drop was about fifteen feet and he made it easily. The French doors were open, and Carter darted into the room before one of the guards in the garden below could see his silhouette.

The room smacked of money, with massive antique

Spanish furniture, thick Oriental and Moroccan carpets on the parquet floors, and original oils on the walls. There were two doors, one to the hall, the other to the bedroom. The one to the bedroom was open.

Carter started that way, when he heard footsteps in the hall. He dived behind a set of ornate screens, and through a crack between them saw the one called Rodesh enter the room carrying a tray.

"Dinner."

"I'm in the bath . . . leave it."

Carter waited until Rodesh had set the tray on a coffee table and exited before he came out from behind the screens. He lifted the fine linen cover from the tray, picked up a roll, and went into the bedroom.

The door to the bath was open. Carter lounged against the jamb and munched on the roll as he watched her rise like a nymph from a sea of bubbles. He admired the long line of her back and the tautness of her bare buttocks before speaking.

"Twenty-four hours and you haven't changed a bit."

She gasped and whirled, anger contorting her lovely face. "Rodesh, you bastard . . . Carter!"

"Bon soir, mademoiselle."

"Thank God you made it."

He tossed her a towel and grabbed a second one to apply to her back.

"Did you ever have any doubts?" he asked lightly.

"Frankly, yes."

"Ah, ye of little faith," he chuckled. "What's up so far? I've nailed three of the four guests. Aflag is keeping some heavy-duty company down there."

"I don't know," she replied. "As usual, I haven't been allowed out of the suite since we arrived. But I did manage to plant a mini-recorder in the library."

"How much tape?"

"An hour and a half, but it's voice activated."

"Terrific. Witten-Jones said you were good."

"Thanks," she said, wrapping the towel around her at last. "What next?"

"We wait. I noticed a bottle of wine on that tray Igor brought up. Want to split it?"

The lights in the sitting room were off. Carter stood in the open French doors, rechecking the passage of the four guards outside. Their routine hadn't changed.

"I'm ready."

Carter turned. She was dressed all in black: skintight slacks, black sweater, and a dark scarf covering her blond hair. Over this she was pulling a floor-length lounge robe.

He went around the bedroom and, one by one, unscrewed all the bulbs in the lamps. Then he moved by Miriam into the bath. He shoved washcloths and tissues down the bowl until he was sure it was plugged. Then he flushed the toilet and jimmied the float.

When he had made the bathroom lights inoperable, he headed for the bathtub. The last thing he did before climbing into the tub was test the rising level of water on the bathroom floor.

"Okay, Miriam, you know what to do."

He slid the shower curtain closed and pulled the piano-wire garrote from his belt. Carefully he folded the tape-wrapped ends in his fingers, and settled back to wait.

From his hiding place he could hear Miriam's voice on the phone in the bedroom.

"Aleve, my loo is overflowing! My loo—the toilet! There's water all over the bathroom floor and it's seeping out into the bedroom! Dammit, I don't know—I'm not a plumber!—And bring a flashlight. Something's wrong with the bathroom and bedroom lights, too!"

He heard the receiver being replaced and the padding of her bare feet going into the sitting room.

It was nearly five minutes before he heard the door open and then slam.

"What is it?"

"I told you, the toilet's overflowing. Did you bring a light?"

"Yes."

Carter smiled when he heard Miriam ask the next question. "Where's Rodesh?"

"In the kitchen, eating with Mikdor."

And then Carter saw the beam of the flash dancing across the shower curtain, and tensed his body.

He gauged the man's position by the light and, when he was sure, threw open the curtain.

Aleve didn't have a chance.

Deftly the Killmaster flipped the wire over his neck and with a yank, brought him upright. At the same time, he pressed his knee in the small of the man's back.

One quick lift, a hard twist, and it was over with a single gurgling sound.

Carter dropped the body and stepped over it. Miriam, Stechkin and grenades in hand, waited by the door. She had put on dark, soft-soled sneakers.

"Is he . . . ?"

"Very. You know what to do."

She nodded, and they both darted into the hall. Miriam crossed it and entered one of the rooms in the front that overlooked the parked cars. Carter went to the rear stairs and descended toward the kitchen.

He cracked the door at the bottom and peered into the room.

Rodesh sat at a table, filling his face with lamb stew. The cook was at the stove, ladling a second helping onto his plate.

Carter eased the safety off the silenced Stechkin. Just as the cook turned and stepped back toward the table, the Killmaster threw the door wide and stepped into the room.

He leveled the weapon and carefully squeezed off two bursts of two shots each as both men clawed for the shoulder rigs at their sides.

Each of them doubled up in turn, then folded to the floor. All four shots had hit home, two apiece, dead center in their chests. Their guns clattered to the floor.

Carter watched unemotionally as they both clawed across the tile toward their hardware. He took a step forward and kicked the guns out of their reach.

By the time he returned from locking the rear door on the inside, the cook had already given up the ghost. Rodesh's eyes were glassy, but his head was up and he was still trying to crawl.

Carter leveled the Stechkin again, but no shot was needed. Before he could squeeze one off, Rodesh coughed once and went still.

Carter holstered the Stechkin, unslung the AK-47, and moved into the long hall that ran the length of the villa. He counted off the doors until he came to the study.

On the other side of the door, he could hear the low rumble of voices. Gently, he tried turning the knob.

Dammit!

It was locked. That killed the element of surprise, but with the AK-47 he probably wouldn't need it anyway.

He stood beside the door, flipped the gun on full automatic, and squeezed. Wood shattered and splinters flew. When he saw the door crack, he hit it with his shoulder and then quickly backed off.

As he suspected, the men inside were armed, and they were alerted at the first burst from the Kalashnikov.

A withering burst of fire erupted through the open door, shattering plaster and a painting across the hall from the Killmaster.

Carter pressed against the wall and waited.

''C'mon, baby, c'mon,'' he hissed. ''You've got the go-ahead!''

Suddenly the night outside the villa erupted with two explosions.

Good girl, Carter thought. He could almost see her standing at the open window, lobbing the two grenades down on the cars below.

He yanked one of the flash grenades from his harness, pulled the pin, and lobbed it into the room. The flash of his arm brought another fusillade of gunfire.

Then the grenade went off, and Carter rolled into the room in the wake of the flash.

He drew a deep breath as he hit the floor and rolled up to one knee, firing.

He was only four feet from a man staggering toward the door, his pants in flames. He must have been standing right over the grenade when it went off.

Carter's first burst stitched him across the middle, nearly cutting him in two and throwing both halves back into the room.

The flash had given way to blinding, choking smoke now, an almost impenetrable wall of gray.

A sound.

Carter shifted the muzzle of the rifle and fired a short burst just as he rolled to another position. A slug splintered wood paneling near his head, and the Killmaster fired randomly at its source.

He saw a figure totter toward him through the dimness, and he put it down with a short five-shot burst.

Again he rolled, this time staying near the floor where the gray fog had started to dissipate. He thought he could make out a couple of figures near the tall front windows. Carefully, he pointed the rifle and loosed a long burst.

There was a scream and a moan. One figure dropped to his knees, clutching his gut. The other started pounding the butt of an automatic against the glass panes.

Just as Carter jumped forward and dropped again to the floor, the man whirled. A slug passed over the Killmaster's head in the general direction of where he had just been.

The man staggered toward him from the window.

It was Hamir Aflag. He had already been hit twice, once

high up in the left shoulder, and once in the left thigh.

He dragged his left leg, and his left arm hung uselessly at his side as he teetered forward. His right arm came upward, the pistol he held zeroing in on Carter.

"Good night, Hamir," Carter hissed.

The automatic rifle barked, and kept barking, until Aflag was a mass of gore against the wall. In death, he slowly slid to the floor, staining the dark wood paneling behind him even darker with his blood.

The gray smoke had cleared enough now to where Carter could see all of the room and the carnage. He moved quickly behind the desk and clawed at books. Three tiers were cleared before he found the mini-recorder.

He pocketed it, jammed a fresh thirty-round magazine in the rifle, and headed for the door.

Just the muzzle of the AK-47 had poked from the door when two slugs slammed into the opposite jamb.

One of the outside guards had gotten in, probably through a side door, since Miriam would be covering the front door and the huge foyer.

Carter crouched, extending his weapon around the corner, and sprayed the hall. There was a scream of pain, but two more blasts came from the other man's gun.

Carter had only winged him.

Should he use the last flash grenade? he wondered.

Yes.

He pulled the pin, counted off the seconds, and flipped it into the hall. When the flash came, the Killmaster closed his eyes tightly and rolled.

The other man was firing wildly and blindly, spraying the hall with random lead. The slugs were hitting the floor and wall all around the door.

Carter guessed the flash had momentarily blinded his adversary.

He was right.

The man had overturned a heavy oak bench and was trying

to hide behind it, with only a machine pistol and his arms showing.

Carter finished the second magazine on the man's arms. Screams filled the hallway, and the machine pistol flew from his mangled hands.

Carter thought the man would give up and play dead.

No such move. He bolted to his feet and clawed a big Webley from the holster at his belt.

Carter already had the Stechkin out of his own holster. The Webley was roaring, but the pain in the man's wounded hands and arms wouldn't allow him aim.

Carter fired, twice. They were quick shots, not particularly well aimed, but with the guard directly in front of him, out in the open and upright, it was hard to miss.

Both slugs caught him high in the left shoulder. He slammed back against the wall, his right hand holding his gun flinging out sideways.

The Killmaster pointed the Stechkin carefully.

The man's eyes opened wide with the horror of sudden realization. His mouth opened as if to beg Carter to hold his fire, but no word actually came.

Carter fired.

The guard stiffened. His entire body flinched at the impact, as lead smashed into the center of his chest, tearing at his ribs, destroying them, then passing into the chest where it cut into his heart.

For almost ten seconds he hung there, looking like a butterfly pinned to a wall. Then, as if in slow-motion, he started to sag downward. His eyes lost their brightness. The lids drooped. The hand still holding the pistol opened and the gun slipped free. Then the body slumped over to its right, slowly at first, then faster and faster. He crumpled to the floor, arms flung over his head, while a rapidly widening pool of blood formed on the floor.

Carter leathered the Stechkin and rammed home his last AK-47 magazine as he ran down the hall to the main foyer. When he hit it, he looked up.

Miriam Lockwood was on the second level of stairs, her Stechkin leveled over the banister with both hands.

"Look out, Nick, there's one . . ."

She never finished. Carter heard the scrape of another guard's boots coming through the door. He whirled, bringing up the automatic rifle.

There was no need to fire. Miriam nailed him cleanly, one in the gut and a second in the top of his head on the way down.

"C'mon!"

She was already halfway down the stairs, taking the last of them three at a time.

"Aflag?"

"Dead," Carter rasped.

"The others?"

"All dead. I got the recorder."

He slid to a halt in a crouch just inside the front door. Miriam imitated him on the other side.

"That's two of the guards. There are two more still out there somewhere," she whispered.

"I know."

Carter waved the muzzle of the AK-47 out the door.

No response.

Cautiously, he peered around the jamb. Miriam had done an excellent job. There were six cars parked in front of the villa. Five of them had been grouped, with a sixth, a gray Mercedes sedan, parked by itself off to the side.

All five of the grouped cars were out of commission, three of them in flames.

"Let's go!"

Carter rolled to the edge of the veranda, with Miriam right behind him.

He passed her the rifle and took her pistol.

"Cover me," he hissed, and took off toward the Mercedes in a crouching run.

Halfway to the car he heard glass break in one of the second-story windows, and then slugs from a machine pistol began kicking up chunks of gravel all around him.

At the same time, he saw a blur of movement come out of the trees to his right. He had no time to get off a shot, but he didn't have to.

The AK-47 barked behind him, and the blur went down with a scream.

Carter rolled around the protective shield of the Mercedes and searched the upper windows.

In the light from the blazing cars, it didn't take long to find the shooter. He stood dead center in the window, waiting for something to aim at.

Carter filled his other hand with his own Stechkin and stretched prone. Four quick shots made the man dive for cover.

"Second story, directly above you! Got it?"

"Got it!" she shouted.

The man's head came up, and Carter peppered the sill all around him.

"Now!"

She came, backpedaling, strafing the window with fire from the rifle. Carter didn't let up either. He kept pumping slugs from the two pistols at any sign of movement.

The AK-47 clicked on empty. Miriam discarded it and dived into the Mercedes behind the wheel.

"Keys?"

"Yes," she replied as the engine roared to life.

Carter sighed in relief. She had said they always left the keys in the cars, just in case a hasty retreat was necessary.

There was no more firing, and no sign of life at the window. Carter fired twice more for good measure as Miriam opened the door on his side.

"Drive!" he growled, leaping into the passenger seat.

The car lurched forward, its rear tires spewing gravel, before Carter could even get the door closed. She hit the arc of the drive in a three-quarter slide, and kept the powerful car floored.

From the shrubbery at the corner of the house, a running figure appeared.

"He must have come down the back stairs . . ."

"Yeah," Carter replied, gauging the distance and seeing the glint of a machine pistol in the man's hand. "He's going to beat us to the curve in the drive."

"I see."

Trees shielded him from them, and them from him, as the big car approached the curve in the drive.

"He'll be waiting just around the curve."

"I know," she said.

"Hit him!" Carter hissed.

He was relieved when he looked across the car and saw her set face in the dashboard lights.

Miriam Lockwood was a professional. Carter knew she wouldn't hesitate for a second.

She hit the curve full tilt in third, pulled the shift lever into second, and headed right toward the crouching figure.

The guard got off one wild burst before the car thudded into his body. The right front tire lifted a foot, and then the right rear.

"Hang on!" she cried, yanking the car back onto the gravel from the lawn.

They were headed for the gates, the speedometer needle nudging sixty.

Ten feet from the gates, they folded over one another in the front seat.

There was an ear-splitting screech of metal and cracking glass. The nose of the car went down and the trunk went up.

They seemed to hang there for an eternity, and then the gates gave and they were sailing through.

"Turn right."

She did and jammed her foot to the carpet. They rocked a few times and then they were sailing. Carter leaned close to her ear.

"You know the area, don't you?" She nodded, and he explained where Yashif was.

"I know it," she shouted. "That road goes all the way up to the edge of the Rif. This one curves around and connects with the coast about five miles over."

"Good. Get there!"

The big car was steaming, and both front tires were nearly flat by the time they reached the turnoff that would lead them back to the coast.

About two miles later, they came out on a wide clearing and a fork in the road. Yashif was waiting, his lights off, the motor running.

"Stop here!"

She did, ten feet from the guardrail. Carter dumped what was left of the hardware and slid from the car. Miriam was already sprinting for the other sedan.

Carter lifted the hood of the Mercedes and, using a sharp stick, jammed the carburetor's throttle wide open. The engine's powerful roar shattered the stillness of the night as he moved around to the driver's side.

Leaving the door open, he used it to brace himself in a crouch on the very edge of the seat. He dropped the shift lever into first, and the car lurched forward with its last gasp of power, hurtling toward a ridge over the sea.

At the last second, Carter sprang free, rolled to his knees, and stood to watch the big car sail out over the water. It seemed to poise in midair like a roaring steel elephant for a second, and then it nosed forward and plummeted into the darkness.

Yashif gunned the car into action the instant Carter's butt hit the rear seat.

"How far to M'diq?"

"Keeping to the speed limit, ten minutes," the Tuareg replied.

"Keep to the speed limit," Carter said. "We've already drawn enough attention."

His gaze shifted to Miriam in the front passenger seat. She was shaking violently.

"Well, I'll be damned," he chuckled. "You are human."

"Only afterward," she replied, managing to smile through chattering teeth.

"How did it go?" Yashif asked.

"Clean sweep," the Killmaster replied, lighting two cigarettes and handing one to Miriam. "How long before the authorities begin massing?"

"An hour," Yashif said.

Carter leaned back in the seat.

In an hour, they would be sailing the Med.

FIVE

Nick Carter tensed when he felt the fingertips touch his shoulder, and relaxed when he opened one eye and saw the old seaman's craggy face.

"We are starting the inward leg. We should be off the coast of Ceuta in about twenty minutes."

Carter nodded, and the old man shuffled from the cabin.

Miriam was sleeping peacefully in the bunk across the aisle. When they had come aboard, she had said that she couldn't sleep; it was obvious that she had changed her mind.

She had unfastened her long silky hair. It now hung around her neck, and a thick section of it draped down over half her face, nearly covering her mouth.

She looked so innocent and peaceful in sleep that it was hard to imagine that she had just helped Carter kill a dozen men.

Suddenly one eye popped open and a smile took shape on her lips. "Time?"

Carter nodded. "About fifteen, twenty minutes."

She was up and alert instantly, reaching for the wet suits they would use to swim into the port of Ceuta.

Five minutes later they were both on deck. Other than the running lights of the fishing boat and the faint lights of Ceuta in the distance, the night was inky black.

Karem, the old boatman, met them at the hatch. "You have memorized the landing spot?"

"We have," Carter nodded. "Your daughter?"

"She will be waiting with clothing. You will stay in her apartment tonight. She has already purchased space for you on the morning hydrofoil to Algeciras."

"A thousand thanks, Karem."

"None are needed. I trust Yashif Beirmaudi that I do the correct deed, and I am paid well. I will tell you when to go over with the light."

He disappeared forward, and Carter joined Miriam at the rail. They were swinging diagonally to the little chunk of Moroccan coastline that still belonged to Spain. Outlines of buildings and houses started to take shape in the distance.

"This is the rough part, isn't it?"

Carter nodded. "I think the Moroccan authorities will nail it as a terrorist kill, especially when they identify the bodies. But that won't stop them from closing off all the frontiers. By getting onto Spanish soil this way, there's no trace."

They were moving in close to land now. Ahead and to his right about three miles, Carter could see the harbor entrance.

There was a brief flash of light from amidships of the boat. It was quickly answered by a flash from shore, about five hundred yards to the left of the harbor.

"That's it," the Killmaster growled, squeezing Miriam's shoulder. "Let's go."

He moved to the edge of the boat, under the rail, and heard her crawling behind him. He didn't hesitate, just shoved his body as far from the boat as he could and let go.

He was falling, out and down, the boat a black, moving mass at his side. He took a bearing on it and the lights, and knew his body was parallel to the water. He twisted, trying to bring his legs around to knife in feet-first.

He was only partially successful, hitting the water at an angle. The life jacket took the brunt of the impact, but it jerked around on his chest, shaking his body as he went under.

He relaxed in the blackness of the water, letting the life jacket return him to the surface. The second he broke the surface he started kicking and stroking to escape the wake of the boat. At that level it was even darker than it had been on deck, but he sensed that he was moving away from the vessel.

He paused, jackknifing in the water to get his bearings. The fishing boat was already a couple of hundred feet away, throttling up, beginning its turn back to the open sea.

He'd made it clean. Now, where was Miriam?

Treading water, he heaved himself above the life jacket's buoyancy. Taking a bearing from the lights ashore, he started to calculate. She would have waited ten seconds or so to make sure she cleared his falling body. That would put her farther along the wake of the boat from Carter's present position. And because of his superior arm and leg strength, she was probably closer to the wake.

"Miriam!"

There was no answer. He estimated the distance, took another bearing on the shore, and began to swim. Every minute or so he heaved himself up out of the water and tried to pierce the blackness.

He swam in circles, widening them at the completion of each one. Minutes passed. He called again, and again, and still there was no answer.

And then, above the normal sounds of the sea and harbor, he heard her far to his right.

"Miriam?"

"Here . . . over here!"

Then he spotted her. She was in a direct line with the shore. He could see her bobbing head outlined against the lights beyond.

He began to swim. As he got nearer he could see her head turning frantically, trying to search him out.

Then she saw him.

"Wait there . . . relax. Roll to your back and let the life jacket do the work!"

And then he reached her.

"Okay?"

"I think so, but I twisted my leg going in. It got doubled up under me."

"But you made it."

"Yeah," she chuckled. "I just closed my eyes and fell off the deck. Ouch!"

He was squeezing up and down her leg under water. "It's your knee, probably just a wrench. It will work itself out. Let's swim."

"God, that shoreline looks like it's on another planet."

Carter squinted his eyes, peering along the coast until he thought he had pinpointed the general area where they had seen the light.

"Ready?"

"Don't I have to be?" she groaned.

"Let's go!"

They began to swim, moving with steady kicks and strokes for ten minutes, then pausing to rest in the water. The clothes they wore beneath their wet suits made movement even more clumsy in the water.

"It's cold."

"You'll get used to it. Keep moving!"

A little over an hour later, they were less than two hundred yards from shore. The lights of the harbor gleamed to their right. Directly in front of them and stretching far to their left were piers with every imaginable kind of small boat tied up.

Carter scrambled until he could get his penlight from beneath the wet suit, and then flashed it toward the shore.

"There . . . to the left!" Miriam cried.

He turned to face her. Her face was a white blob against the darkness of the water. "Can you make it?"

"I'm beat."

"Then get some reserve," he said. "It's only another five minutes, ten at the most."

It took fifteen."

"Here, and watch the rocks!" It was a female voice, and it came from an open area just to their left.

Carter grabbed Miriam's arm and pulled her close to him. Then he side-stroked them in until their feet found solid rock. They waded the rest of the way to shore, and a figure materialized out of the darkness.

"Laeila?"

"Yes. This way!"

They followed her up the beach to the shelter of a fisherman's small warming shed. She fumbled in a pile of nets and gear until she came up with a suitcase.

"Put your wet suits in here, and hurry. A jeep patrol comes along here every hour from the Spanish garrison. They check for smuggling."

Carter and Miriam quickly peeled off the wet suits and stuffed them into the bag.

"This way—my car is over there."

It was a Renault 5, and she handled it like a champ. They breezed through the main part of town into the Moroccan quarter, and within fifteen minutes of coming ashore pulled up in front of an old, crumbling three-story building.

Without a word they followed her into the building and up to the third floor.

The apartment was only one small room, but it was clean and warm. To Carter, the wide, low bed looked like heaven.

"There is food. The bath is there . . . small, I'm afraid."

"It's wonderful," Miriam enthused.

The girl pulled a second suitcase from beneath a dresser. "There are clothes in here for both of you. The fit may be a little snug, but they will pass you off as tourists on the hydrofoil.''

"What time?''

"It leaves at seven-thirty sharp in the morning from the maritime pier. You can get a taxi on the corner.'' She turned to leave.

"Laeila, wait.''

"Yes?''

"This is your apartment?''

"Yes, but do not worry.'' She smiled shyly. "I will stay with my boyfriend tonight. Good-bye . . . and good luck.''

Then she was gone and they stood awkwardly staring at each other and the room.

"One bed,'' Carter commented.

"I noticed. Probably only one shower, too.''

Carter grinned. "Want to share both of them?''

Watching each other shed their clothes was like an act of absolution. It seemed to drain away the tension and danger they had just been through.

Together they moved into the tiny bath. Carter adjusted the shower and turned to face her.

Her mussed blond hair curled about her face, softening her features. Her breasts jutted full and heavy from her body, and the lines of her hips and thighs were clean and perfect.

They both took one step and met, flesh to naked flesh. Her thighs against his and her breasts against his chest were warm and soft.

Her head tilted back and her eyes closed as her lips parted. Then their mouths were glued together. He held her fast against him and she increased the pressure that he started.

"Shower?''

"Yes,'' he whispered, "a quick one.''

"No,'' she murmured, "slow. Very slow.''

They stepped into the shower. Carter cracked the bar of soap in half and handed one piece to her.

Her lips smiled, but there was no humor in her eyes. "Do you think we're sick?"

"No, just not quite normal."

"I mean, after . . ."

"I know what you mean. Scrub."

They lathered one another, and then caressed the lather. Carter turned her around, moving in behind her until their bodies touched, and washed her front. When she began shaking, he reversed the position and she performed the same magic for him.

They patted each other dry with huge towels, and then moved into the bedroom.

"Bed?" she said.

"Soon."

He stepped in front of her and slid his forearms under hers so that his palms cupped her elbows. He drew her to him. Miriam kept her face turned down slightly, as though she might be a bit afraid. This unusual shyness turned Carter on all the more.

He kissed her forehead, then her eyes. Her face raised a little, and his lips contacted her smooth skin. When her mouth at last came up and met his, she seemed as impatient as he.

Her arms slipped under his, around his waist, and his went around her shoulders. Their bodies met with an electric jolt that brought him at once to full sexual tension, and he became aware of each area and curve of her body against him, the soft, yielding breasts, her stomach, her legs, her pelvis, rubbing against his.

They held each other tightly, their mouths working hotly against each other, and they swayed slightly.

Without parting, they fell to the bed.

"I should warn you . . ." she whispered.

"About what?"

"I get a little crazy."

"Don't worry about it. I'll join you."

His hand went back to her lush breasts, lifting, rolling, stroking, and her breathing grew rapid. When both of her arms tightened around him, he released her breasts and caressed her legs, then up over her thighs.

He wrapped his arms around her, caressing her body to his, holding her tightly as they kissed. Her snaking tongue probed the recesses of his mouth to let him know how ready she was. He softly rubbed her back and shoulders, then slowly massaged his way lower, lower. His hands filled with her firm, full buttocks.

Her legs parted and she managed to somehow squirm beneath him.

"Now . . . there . . ." she sighed, and lifted to meet his thrust. "Do everything," she moaned, her body writhing under him. "Everything!"

And he did, everything that made her wild, that created the metamorphosis that turned her from a purring kitten to a growling, clawing jungle cat.

He did it all, until she arched toward him, urging him with every gesture and sound.

Slowly, and together, in matching rhythms they moved, each sensing the rising tumult of passion in the other until their bodies were whirlpools of frenzied motion.

Suddenly, with her nails digging into his straining back, Miriam arched and strained as though her whole body were one long, intense, taut string that was about to snap.

And then it did, and he with her.

It began with a low roar in his chest and mounted to a piercing shout as his whole being burst forth like a torrent inside him. At the same time, she screamed, locking herself against him, driving herself to fulfillment.

Both their bodies settled in occasional spasms and convulsive murmurs as they completely drained the lust from each other. Slowly he slid the dead weight from her body as she caressed his face and hair.

"Tomorrow?" she whispered.

"London," he said. "I can check in from there, and be debriefed there as well as Washington."

"I was hoping you'd say that."

SIX

Norman Dufont stepped into Regent Street, defying traffic with his umbrella. On the far curb, he saluted a cursing cabdriver with the instrument, and jauntily entered the Piccadilly Hotel.

Heads turned as he moved across the lobby toward the desk. The attention he attracted was not particularly because of his appearance, even though he was immaculately attired. It was more his manner: unmitigated arrogance.

Dufont was around average height, heavily built, with a head of thick black hair and heavy black eyebrows above deep-set, hooded brown eyes.

It was his military gait and the set of his stern features that gave him an air of arrogance. It was his eyes that marked him as a man of purpose.

Norman Dufont was a man of mysterious fortune, an avid environmentalist, a rabid antiwar activist, an avowed "dove," and, since the age of eighteen, one of the most brilliant KGB operatives in England.

"Nine-twelve, please."

"Yes, sir. Oh, a message, sir. It's marked 'Urgent.' "

Dufont quickly scanned the piece of paper.

It was only a phone number, in the Kensington area of London. No message other than the word "urgent" was needed. Dufont knew the number well.

He didn't even bother going to his room. He darted into one of the lobby telephone booths and dialed.

"Yes?"

"Sir Marcus, Norman Dufont here."

"Thank God. I've been trying to reach you all morning. Have you heard the telly or read the papers?"

"As a matter of fact, yes."

Sir Marcus Loring's voice on the phone had a strange quivering quality in it. It was unlike the blustering old aristocrat to stammer or falter in his thoughts or speech. Dufont recognized the sounds as animal fear.

"My God, man, how can you be so calm? Pierre is dead!"

"I know he is, Sir Marcus."

"They must be on to us. They're going all out. Obviously the killer was a professional."

"Poppycock," Dufont hissed. "Aflag and those other three had enemies all over the world. Pierre Delamaine was just in the wrong place at the wrong time, that's all. It was a coincidence, nothing more."

"Nevertheless, Red Star will have to be called off."

"What?"

"That's right, call it off. The committee agrees with me that right now it would be just too risky. With Pierre being killed with those men, the authorities are sure to put two and two together. We'll have to call it off and wait until their guard is down."

"Sir Marcus, that would be very difficult. Once an operation like this has started, it is very difficult to stop it."

Dufont checked his watch: noon.

Good Christ, he thought, *the teams are already in place.* Everything was timed to the second to begin at 3 P.M. sharp. It couldn't be called off.

Loring's nervous voice brought him back.

"Besides, without the cooperation of one of these foreign underground units, where will we be able to keep them? How will we get them out of the country?"

"I have an alternate plan, Sir Marcus. I have always had such a plan, just in case."

"You? You have a plan? Dammit, man, why haven't I been told about it? You would think that you were the head of the organization instead of me! How dare you . . ."

"It was," Dufont said, doing his best to keep the tenseness out of his voice, "a plan that I did not want to use. That is the reason I never mentioned it to you."

Pause. Silence.

"I just don't want the two of them harmed. I mean, I certainly don't agree with their policies, but I don't want them harmed!"

"Every precaution will be taken, Sir Marcus. I'll tell you what . . . can you meet me in a half hour in the Bloomsbury flat? I'll explain everything to you then."

"Very well. But in the meantime, I want you to postpone the operation. All right?"

"Of course, Sir Marcus."

"I have your word on it?"

"My word, Sir Marcus."

"A half hour."

The line went dead. Dufont got a tone and dialed another number.

"Hello?"

He dropped sufficient coins, and spoke. "Carla, Norman . . ."

"I've been waiting for your call. My God, it's all over the papers and the television! What happened?"

"My guess is that it was a professional hit, probably against Aflag. The timing was just inopportune for us, that's all. Sir Marcus is in quite a tiff."

A laugh. "I'll just bet the old walrus is."

"He wants to call Red Star off."

"Impossible!"

"Of course it's impossible. But we'll have to risk accommodating our two boarders ourselves. I'll arrange guards from the organization so our people won't be involved."

"Will Sir Marcus and the committee agree?"

"I can handle the committee. They'll be too frightened to do a damned thing. As for Sir Marcus . . ."

"Yes?"

"I'm meeting him in a half hour in the Bloomsbury flat. Can you reach the cleaners?"

"I believe so." A short pause. "Is that the only way?"

"I do believe it is."

"They will be there."

Dufont took the elevator to the suite he rented year round. In the bath, he fumbled beneath the old-fashioned claw-footed tub he had had installed the previous year. A steel drawer slid on well-oiled hinges from the tub's false bottom.

In the drawer was a broken-down Beretta Model 12 sub-machine gun, an Uzi sniper rifle with a laser sight, and three 9mm Beretta pistols with silencers.

He slid one of the pistols into a special pocket of his trench coat, then anchored the silencer to his right leg inside his highly polished Italian leather boot.

He glanced at his watch. It was 12:10.

He would just make the appointment with Sir Marcus.

Mildred Hastings, senior MP from south Devon, pushed her breakfast tea tray to the foot of the bed and glared at the clock.

It was nearly twelve-thirty. What a disgustingly decadent time to arise, even on a Sunday morning, she thought. But then the cocktail party the evening before had turned into a political forum and had not broken up until three o'clock that morning.

The phone rang, and was quickly picked up by her house-keeper in the kitchen of her Mayfair apartment.

Mildred swung her legs over the side of the bed and heaved her tired old body to her feet.

Tired? Yes.

Old? Never.

She was fifty-five years young, and in the prime of her life.

But she did admit to the tiredness. Being the voice of Conservative causes and a hearty foe of disarmament in Parliament for the past twelve years was very taxing.

And now, being forced to muster all her energy almost every hour since these new American missiles had been implemented was taking more and more out of her.

She remembered the argument at the party the night before between herself and that pompous ass, Sir Marcus Loring, and his two toadies.

By the end of it, she had accused Sir Marcus and his radical organization of being a bunch of rich dilettantes who would invite the Russians to tea within the hour after they had overrun the country.

That was wrong, she knew, but Sir Marcus was such a strutting poppinjay and such a horrid example of the idle rich who used otherwise legitimate causes to bolster their own egos, that she couldn't resist it.

"Madam?"

"Yes, Gertrude?"

"Your hairdresser, madam. He would like to know if he can come at three instead of four."

"François? How odd, he's always come every Sun-day. . ."

"His relatives, madam."

"Oh, very well. What difference will an hour make?"

"Will you need anything else, madam?"

"What? . . . Oh, no, Gertrude. I'll see you in the morn-ing. Is my bath drawn?"

"Yes, madam."

In the bathroom, Mildred Hastings dropped her nightdress to the floor and stopped momentarily in front of the mirror.

"Not bad," she chuckled, "for an old warmonger."

Major General Sir John Hillary carefully checked the lures in the brim of the battered hat before placing it on his head. He wouldn't be using a single one of them—live bait was the rule this day—but he liked to sport the lures.

On vacation, the lures were the same to Sir John as his nine rows of campaign ribbons were when he was on duty in Brussels.

Now, after seeing to the last American missile installation in Europe, Sir John was on vacation in his beloved Cornwall, and he meant to enjoy it to the utmost.

"Gladys?"

"Yes, dear?"

"The best fisherman in Cornwall is off. Be back by teatime."

"Shall I send down for you if the telephone rings with an international crisis?" she teased.

"Send all you want!" he roared. "I shall be sufficiently hidden among the coves so no one will find me!"

"Teatime then, darling."

Sir John opened the front door of the cottage and drank in the fresh clean smell of the sea and the wild jagged cliffs of the south Cornwall coast.

"God's country," he sighed, and started down the path at a brisk pace.

He followed the cliff lane for nearly a mile, and then cut off by Alder's Tea Shop toward the beach.

Old Garvey Alder stood at the door of his tearoom, clouds of smoke billowing from the huge bowl of his pipe.

"Bit of a wind today, Yer Honor."

"There is, Garvey. Where will they be biting?"

"South cove, I'd say. Off the point."

"I'll try it."

"Good luck to ya, Yer Honor."

"Thank you, Garvey."

By the time Sir John hit the beach and turned south, a small blond man in a heavy pea jacket had paid his bill and was hurrying after him.

Sir Marcus Loring paused at the second-floor landing and cursed the fact that the old Bloomsbury brownstone was without an elevator. When the lease was up, he would make sure that the next apartment they secured for the organization's clandestine meetings would not be a fourth-floor walk-up.

Sir Marcus was fifty-nine years old, five-feet-nine-inches tall, and weighed 340 very blubbery pounds. He had given up such strenuous exercise as walking up stairs thirty years before.

Mopping perspiration from his face and neck, he grunted to a start and huffed and puffed his way up the final two flights.

He had a key to the apartment, but he tried the door first. He was late. Considering Dufont's fetish for punctuality, the man was probably already there.

The door was unlocked.

"Sir Marcus, good to see you, sir." Norman Dufont, subservient as usual to a man of higher rank, assisted Loring's bloated physique to a chair. "A drink?"

"Thank you, Dufont. Yes, a gin, please."

"A gin it is."

Loring studied the younger man as he fussed at the makeshift bar. Proper dress, definitely, he thought, and good bearing, probably regimental background, he didn't know for sure. But in the time Sir Marcus had known the man, he had decided that there was something very un-British about him. Just what it was, he hadn't as yet been able to put his finger on.

"Here you are, Sir Marcus."

Loring accepted the drink as he would from a servant, with a grunt and nod.

"You have followed my orders and canceled Red Star?"

"Of course, Sir Marcus."

"Good." He sipped the gin, belched, and spoke again. "Perhaps we should cancel altogether. I never really approved of the theory in the first place, you know."

"I know, Sir Marcus, but we all agreed."

"Coerced would be a better word. I didn't really mean for the People's Party for Peace to become a terrorist organization when I founded it, you know."

Of course you didn't, you fat pig. You founded it because your peers in Parliament rejected you, and you wanted a platform to gain prestige and status with the press.

"It's this new breed coming into the party, radicals, any means to achieve an end. Could be very dangerous."

Dufont sipped his own drink and suppressed a frown. He knew that Loring was alluding to Carla, and himself, and the younger members Dufont had brought in.

The old man was like that. He would belittle you right to your face, as if you were a third person and not even present.

"Dangerous, extreme measures are sometimes needed, Sir Marcus, to further a cause."

"Yes, yes, so you have often said. But kidnapping? God, what have we come to!"

"We have come to the realization that lesser means will no longer work," Dufont replied, unable to keep all the sarcasm out of his voice.

"I daresay *you* have," Loring wheezed, holding out his glass. "I haven't. Another gin."

Dufont took the glass and moved to the bar, glancing down at the Rolex on his wrist.

The cleaners would arrive in five minutes.

"I think you must admit that, since I joined the party, organization has improved one-hundred percent."

"Yes, yes."

"And recruitment has been up ten-fold."

"That's true, Dufont, but my people tell me that new party members in Italy, France, and Germany have been drawn heavily from terrorist organizations in those countries."

"It's impossible to fully screen all the applicants, Sir Marcus. And besides, the kind of men and women you speak of do come in handy now and then. Witness the precise planning and execution of Red Star."

"Well, we shall never know now, shall we? You're taking a devilishly long time to make a drink, old man."

"We will know, very soon, how Red Star works, you fat old pig," Dufont murmured.

"What's that you say . . . ?" Loring wheezed.

From beneath a layer of linen napkins on the bar, Dufont withdrew the silenced Beretta. He turned and walked back toward Loring.

"I'm saying, Sir Marcus, that Red Star is on, and you're out."

"Good grief, man, what—"

Dufont fired with the barrel of the silencer six inches from Sir Marcus Loring's head. The slug entered his brain directly between the eyes at an upward slant. It had been point-drilled but only slightly, just enough to spread, but not enough to completely pierce the back of the skull and create a mess.

There was a single spurt of blood, and the impact had thrown the head back so that it was absorbed by the front of Sir Marcus's shirt and vest.

"Clean, very clean, if I do say so myself."

Dufont righted the body to make sure it wouldn't topple and drip on the rug, and then he moved to answer the light rap on the door.

"Cleaners."

"Come in!"

There were three of them. They didn't even glance at the corpse in the chair as they went about dismantling the drapes from the windows. They left the sheers and wrapped the body in the drapes, quickly and efficiently, the entire process not taking over three minutes.

"We'll have them back by tomorrow afternoon," one of the men said as they reached the door.

"Very good. Cheerio."

"Cheerio, sir."

Dufont freshened his drink and turned on the television. He would nap here, in the apartment. This was as good a place as any to wait until it was time to pick up Carla.

Carter lay back against the rocks and let the rare English sun bake his near naked body.

Lyme Regis, on the south Dorset coast—expensive and tasteful luxury. He would have never dreamed.

They had flown into London in the afternoon two days earlier. Separately, they had filed their reports, been debriefed, and Miriam had turned in the tape.

"What are your orders?"

"Hang tight for a few days," Carter replied. "If nothing comes up on this side of the pond, go home."

"Good. I have a little place down south. Care to join me?"

"Love to."

The "little place" turned out to be a nine-room cottage that would have been an exquisite villa on the south coast of France. It sported a maid, a cook, a Bentley in the garage, Aubusson rugs on the floor, and twenty-two-year-old scotch in the bar.

The first evening's dinner was chateaubriand with béarnaise sauce and strawberries with thick Devon cream. These delicacies were washed down with Mouton-Rothchild and a superb vintage champagne. Then they went to bed and made love on perfumed satin sheets.

"I didn't know you were rich."

"I'm not, just comfortable. My parents put a bit by for me before they passed away."

"With all this, why did you go into the service?"

"I dislike croquet, bridge, and cocktail parties, and I'm good at what I do. Does it bother you that I have money?"

"Not me."

The love was superb, the ocean calming, and the sun a blessing.

"Are you asleep?"

One eye opened. "Yes. I'm dreaming of a wet, honey-haired goddess with huge breasts and nymphomaniacal tendencies."

"I'll check the local pubs," she laughed, and dropped onto the blanket beside him. "Lovely spot, isn't it?"

"It is. And so are you."

He rolled to his side and took her in his arms.

"Miss Lockwood . . . I say, Miss Lockwood . . ."

Carter unhanded her and they both rolled their eyes up toward the top of the rocks. The housekeeper stood, outlined against the prim houses of Lyme Regis and the Dorset cliffs beyond.

"Yes, Lettie?"

"A call from London, miss. They must speak to you right away. They left a number."

Their eyes met. "Damn," she said.

"Double damn," he replied, and folded the blanket.

They hurried, out of habit, hand in hand, through the narrow, winding steep streets to the cottage. Carter built two drinks while Miriam made the call.

It was a short one.

"The tape was dynamite. They want us both in London as soon as possible."

"How much dynamite?"

"Evidently a lot. Your brass has flown over on the Concorde to meet my brass. They're using Sir Richard Witten-Jones's yacht on the Thames to assemble, in case our office entrances are being watched."

"Must be *very* big."

"We'll take the Bentley to London. They want us to get to the yacht separately."

"Damn," Carter hissed.

"Double damn," she replied.

SEVEN

Bloody nuisance, Sir John thought, casting expertly and watching as the weighted hook dropped just beyond the cresting waves. In fact, two bloody nuisances.

One was the sleek, L-type Royal Navy surplus power launch. It had arrived shortly after he had made his way down to the cove. At first it had trolled up and down well beyond the breakwater. But in the last half hour it had come closer and closer to shore.

Blighters, he raged, *got the whole bloody coastline to troll in, mostly empty at that. And they have to muck up the south cove.* Another five minutes and they would directly interfere with his cast.

The second nuisance was the young journalist who now hunkered down among the rocks five yards behind him.

"*Devon Star,* Sir John. I don't mean to muck up your fishing—"

"Then go away, young man."

"As the new co-commander of NATO, our readers would like to hear your personal feelings about the American missiles in England and on the Continent."

Sir John had been stonewalling the lad for the better part of an hour, but he refused to give up and leave.

Odd chap, Sir John thought. *Dresses like a bloody merchantman, and even though he says the right words in the right order, his accent states his class.*

"You there, can't you troll a bit farther out? You get any closer and you'll damn well foul my line!"

The three men on the launch acted as though they hadn't heard a word he said. The boat continued its progress toward shore.

"Obstinate buggers, aren't they?"

"They are that," Sir John replied, and then realized that the blond man had left his perch among the rocks and was now standing right at his elbow.

"Look, lad, I'm on holiday. Why don't you leave me be?"

"Can't do that, Sir John."

"Tell you what. Let me have my afternoon of peace, and I'll meet you in the tea room at ten in the morning and give you an interview."

The launch had bowed in to a sandy patch just below and to the left of the point. The pilot had jumped and held the bow fast. The two fishermen who had been trolling off the stern had also jumped off, and were now walking up toward the point.

Something was wrong; Sir John could feel it, almost see it in the men's stern, flat-faced expressions. Their eyes never left his, and their path was directly toward where he sat.

Sir John had been in the midst of too many battles not to recognize the enemy.

Suddenly they both leaped for him. Sir John came to his feet, intending to meet the lunge head-on, when he felt strong fingers at the base of his neck. His head was pulled forward until his face was mashed against the chest of one of the oncoming men.

"Go to sleep, Sir John," the blond reporter said.

Sir John Hillary struck out at the men but missed. The two

in front of him grabbed his arms as he felt something rake his neck on both sides below the ears.

Bloody fools, Sir John thought, *do they think they can take me with mere biting and scratching?*

With a tremendous surge, he freed his arms and pushed away one of the men with his shoulder. At the same time, he lashed out with his booted foot and caught the other in the stomach.

They fell away, and Sir John grabbed for the scratching hands encircling his neck. His fingers closed over cold metal, and in the fleeting second that he was able to release the stranglehold, he caught a glimpse of two massive rings adorning the blond man's index fingers.

Sir John whirled. He lunged at the man and managed to fold his fingers around the lapels of the pea jacket.

Suddenly his fingers stopped working. Then his legs and knees seemed to be leaving his body.

"Damn . . . damn . . ."

"Don't fight it, you old goat."

He staggered. His spine seemed to be turning to jelly. He tried to lift his arms, and realized that they were already lifted. But he couldn't locate his hands.

Insolently, a wet palm was shoved in his face and he reeled across the rocks. He hit his hip . . . or his shoulder . . . he wasn't sure. Then all of him hit the ground.

His mind was working, alive, but his body was dead.

Silence, like a tomb, seemed to go on for hours. He could see a watch on his wrist. It had been one minute.

"Crusty old bastard, ain't he?"

"Got a kick like a mule, he has."

"Come along, lads, into the launch with him. We've got a bit to go to meet the freighter by midnight."

The skeleton clock in its glass dome tinkled the hour melodiously as Mildred Hastings swooped through the foyer and opened the door.

"Ah, François, I'm . . . you're not François . . ."

"No, madam. I am very sorry, but François was forced at the last moment to return to Paris. A serious illness in his family."

He was a short little man with a long, emaciated face and one of those terrible, spiky, punk-rock hairdos, the color of which almost matched his vivid blue eyes. He was wearing a purple silk shirt with a very fancy collar and cuffs, and sky-blue skintight pants.

"Who are you?" Mildred huffed, not entirely pleased with the vision that stood in her very tastefully appointed foyer.

"I am Astelle."

"Estelle?"

"*A*stelle, madam," he corrected archly. "François thinks very highly of me."

"Ah, of course. Well, won't you come in?"

"Merci."

As he floated by her, his slightly glossed lips spread in a toothy smile. She also noticed that a golden earring dangled from the lobe of his left ear.

He paused to pose in the center of the living room. "Where are you usually done, madam?"

"I have a chair, in the master bath."

"Of course."

He followed her with mincing steps into the bath and began to unpack the tools of his trade from a small satchel.

Out of habit, Mildred started to unbutton her blouse, and paused.

Another dazzling smile.

Oh, well, what the hell, she thought. *At least I know he's not the sort to attack women!*

His hands were very gentle and soothing as he worked the shampoo into her hair. In fact, her only complaint was his jewelry. He wore a large ring on each index finger. They kept banging against her ears.

"I say . . ."

"Astelle."

"Astelle, would you mind removing those rings?"

"I would mind very much, madam."

It was his voice that warned her. Suddenly it had gone down a full octave to a very masculine baritone.

She started to raise her head from beneath the faucet, when she felt the skin on both sides of her neck being clawed.

"Damn you!" she cried, and lurched to her feet.

She was a good three inches taller than he and probably a few pounds heavier. But his strength was remarkable. He hung on her neck like a leech, and she couldn't seem to shake him off.

And then she started to fade. Her legs gave way and she felt herself being lowered back to the stool.

Her head was pushed back under the tap and her hair rinsed. A towel was wrapped around her head. She heard his voice as her arms were pushed into her blouse.

"Least I can do fer you, ma'am . . . make you decent."

The blouse was buttoned, and his hands seemed to linger at her breasts.

"Bloody firm ones you got there fer a bird yer age."

The front bell made him scurry to the door. "Yes?"

"Cleaners."

"She's in the bathroom. This way."

He led the two men in white coveralls into the bath. They picked Mildred Hastings up and carried her into the bedroom. The hairdresser helped them take down the bedroom drapes.

"Any trouble at the servants' entrance?"

"Nah. They're used to the likes of us comin' an' goin'. These rich ones is always needin' service of some kind. Told the doorman we was workin' Sundays to keep up with the demands of the likes of this one."

Rolled in the drapes, Mildred Hastings was deposited in a hamper cart in the hall and rolled away.

Fifteen minutes later, the hairdresser was packed up and gone, locking the door behind him.

By the time François rang the bell at Mildred Hastings's Mayfair apartment at his usual weekly time, Mildred was in the back of a van, speeding south toward the Plymouth docks.

He stood for ten solid minutes ringing the bell and angrily stomping his foot.

"Bloody bitch," he said at last, managing to say it in his acquired French accent. "Makes me come on Sunday and then goes out herself. Bloody bitch!"

He rang for another two minutes, and then headed for the elevator, hoping that the tall blond he had just seen in a nearby pub was still dawdling over his beer.

Miriam halted the Bentley three blocks from the AXE apartment at Carter's request. He stepped out onto Charing Cross Road and waved. She mimed a kiss with her lips and tooled the big car west to her own London apartment in Belgravia.

He walked up Charing Cross, cut into a small Soho lane with windows full of female flesh, and found the familiar doorway. There were four apartments—two front, two rear—on the third floor. None of them was marked, and all of them could be opened with the same plasticard key.

Only six men in the world held cards that would open the doors. Nick Carter, AXE N3, was one of them.

He slid what looked like an innocuous Eurobank credit card into the slot, and the door rolled inward. Just inside the door was a small shag rug. Beneath the rug was a pressure pad that, when stepped on, would set off an alarm in London's central AXE headquarters. There were also static- and heat-sensing alarms throughout the apartment.

Carter ran his fingers along the frame of a wall mirror to his right, found the alarm master, and cut it off.

It was four-thirty. They had made excellent time on the drive up from Lyme Regis. Carter's designated time of arrival at the Battersea Bridge landing was six o'clock.

Plenty of time.

The apartment consisted of two rooms, a kitchenette, and a small bath. Nothing fancy, but it didn't need to be . It served as a home away from home for agents in the field. AXE had similar safe houses in all the major cities of the world.

Carter stripped, showered, and freshened his shave. The closet contained four complete different wardrobes. Three of them belonged to three other AXE agents. Carter didn't even know their names.

From his own section he selected a dark, all-season pin-striped suit. It was an off-the-rack suit, but it had been carefully altered to accommodate the bulge made by Wilhelmina's shoulder rig.

The bottom drawer of a huge dresser was his. He selected clean underwear, an off-white shirt, and a conservative tie.

By 5:20 he was dressed and back on the street headed for Leicester Square. He took the tube to Victoria Station. He cabbed from there to Battersea Bridge and strolled down Cheyne Walk to the designated pier.

The yacht was seventy-five feet of muted, floating luxury. It commanded its own slip, and the only sign of security was a ship's officer in crisp whites.

Carter identified himself and stepped aboard. Few lights were on, so he was practically on top of Gig Clark before he saw him.

"Nick, congratulations."

"Thanks," Carter said, shaking the other man's hand.

Clark was one of the pair. The other was Neil Griffen. They were David Hawk's principal aides and bodyguards. The head of AXE went nowhere without them, not even home at night to his Arlington condo, much less abroad.

"Hawk wanted me to warn you. We've lifted just what we need off the tape. None of the gentlemen inside knows where or how the tape was secured. We want to leave it like that."

"Of course. It picked up all the action after the talk?"

Clark nodded and chuckled. "It sounded like World War

Three. Their side was briefed by Miss Lockwood.''

"It was, for about ten minutes.''

Clark handed him to a ship's steward who led him below-decks.

Irish linen, bone china, and antique silver decorated the long table in the owner's salon. Carter guessed that Sir Richard Witten-Jones lived equally well ashore as he did in this floating palace.

Sir Richard himself was seated near the head of the table. He looked up and nodded as Carter entered. Miriam was beside him, dressed in a sedate skirt, blouse, and jacket that on anyone else would have looked dowdy.

She said hello with just her eyes, and the steward seated him at the opposite end of the salon.

Even though the table was set for a banquet, it appeared that only coffee and tea was being served.

Carter requested coffee and checked out the guest list. It was impressive.

Representatives of the Home Office, the Foreign Office, and Defense were there in force. Sir Richard was obviously repping MI6, the foreign intelligence service.

Only a rep from MI5, Britain's internal counterintelligence service, was missing to give the group a full quorum.

That was quickly rectified.

There were two empty chairs at the head of the table. A door opened to the left of the table, and the two chairs were quickly occupied. One by David Hawk, his iron jaw clamped severely around a dead cigar. The other by Sir Maxwell Groot, First Deputy Director of MI5.

"Gentlemen, Miss Lockwood . . . I think you all know David Hawk.'' There was a polite murmur, and Sir Maxwell continued. "Mr. Hawk and Mr. Carter are here because it was their American agency, in a joint mission with our own Six, who chanced upon some interesting information. Carpenter!''

One of the stewards left his post and stepped to a console.

"This is an edited tape that was secured a few days ago during an operation quite unaffiliated. Go ahead."

The machine was turned on. The sound of scraping chairs, coughs, and clinking glasses filled the room through the console's speakers, and then the sound of heavily accented male voices.

"We will speak French, my friends, out of deference to our French friend. May I present Monsieur Pierre Delamaine."

"I assume," Sir Maxwell interjected, "that everyone here is fluent in French?"

There was a chorus of agreement, and the taped voices took over again.

"Concerning our earlier agreements about the materials you have requested, the shipments will be made as per my contract's promises. It is the method of reimbursement that I would like to discuss."

"We have agreed to pay in cash. What is the problem?"

"No problem, I assure you. Mr. Delamaine would like the services of one of your organizations. In return for that service, the people he represents are willing to pay the entire cost of the arms you have requested."

Carter lit a cigarette. He didn't know who Pierre Delamaine was, but he recognized the voice of the principal speaker as Hamir Aflag.

"Soon, very soon, an operation code-named Red Star will take place in England. Two very highly placed U.K. officials will be kidnapped. The means of spiriting them out of the country has already been established."

"Then what do you need us for?"

"An underground organization with loyal followers is needed to keep the two individuals mentioned sequestered until the demands for their release can be met."

"Just how important are these Englishmen?"

"Very highly placed . . . two people that the government in the U.K., as well as the U.S., cannot afford to lose."

"That will make it a bit difficult, keeping them on ice."

"It will. That is why Monsieur Delamaine's fee is so generous. So, gentlemen, what is your—"

The tape went blank. Carter smiled. That must have been the point where the AK-47 in his hands had started tearing the door apart.

"There you have it, gentlemen, Miss Lockwood. We have every reason to believe that this operation Red Star is not a hoax. It is probably going full-steam ahead at this very moment." Sir Maxwell turned to the man beside him. "Mr. Hawk."

Hawk leaned forward, placed his elbows on the table, and made a production out of removing the cigar from his lantern jaw.

"Several years ago, one of your own, Sir Marcus Loring, formed an anti-nuclear-arms, antiwar group called the People's Party for Peace. When it was learned that the organization had gone international, MI5 passed it along to MI6, who in turn brought in our CIA and the French *Direction de la Surveillance du Territoire*.

"Known members—at that time there were few—were kept under catch-as-catch-can surveillance. They weren't considered radical or strong enough in numbers for more than that."

"Who is this Delamaine?" asked the Home Office.

"I'll get to that. Up until about a year ago, this Peace Party did little more than demonstrate and make a lot of noise. It was about then, a year ago, that the group took on better organization. Their ranks all over the world began to swell, and they evidenced a very militant core."

Here Sir Maxwell took over again. "Much of the militancy was internal sabotage, fire bombings, threats, and even a few robberies for funding. We began to pay more attention to them, and discovered that they had been highly infiltrated by KGB-trained operatives."

"Who are these operatives?"

"This we don't know, and obviously have to find out

before Red Star takes effect. Pierre Delamaine was the head of the French branch of the People's Party. Obviously, he was at the meeting you just heard as their representative.''

Suddenly the tension in the room was heavy. British intelligence, both at home and abroad, was often castigated for its "old boy" network. But there were times when the close-knit old school ties of these men proved to be advantageous.

"I shall put Special Branch and Scotland Yard on immediate alert.''

"Extra security for the P.M.?"

"Of course.''

"Seal off ports and airports.''

"That has been done.''

"Has Sir Marcus been picked up for questioning?''

"A fire team is turning England upside down looking for him now. He is not at his country house, and his Belgravia flat is empty. We have teams watching both.''

"What about the other known members?''

"Under close surveillance. So far, nothing.''

"My guess is that they would use hired thugs to do the actual dirty work.''

At last Sir Maxwell stood, waving the others to silence.

"We will be code-named Interrupt. Central headquarters are being set up right now in Cavendish Square. Coordinate all your people and have them check in there as soon as possible.''

"Going to be bloody rough when we don't even know who they're after.''

"That's the point,'' Sir Maxwell said. "When they move, we'll have to jump, fast.''

The various men stood and left. They would fan out across London to their respective offices, and the machinery would gear up.

Carter hoped it would be fast enough. He guessed that it wouldn't.

Hawk spoke with his eyes, telling Carter to stay put.

Sir Richard and Miriam Lockwood had also remained in their seats, as did Hawk and Sir Maxwell. When the room was cleared, Sir Maxwell spoke.

"Five and Six will work together on this, Sir Richard?"

"Of course."

"I will coordinate our people here in England with our foreign agents," Hawk said, and turned to Carter. "We have decided that you and Miss Lockwood should stay with this, N3. By free-lancing, you might come up with something that a mass of men running hither, thither, and yon could miss."

"Of course, sir. I have a lot of contacts in the London underworld."

"We know that," Sir Maxwell replied. "And Miriam has several contacts in society that might unearth Sir Marcus's recent acquaintances."

"Good luck to you both," Hawk growled.

"Good luck to us all," Sir Richard added.

It was a sign to move. Carter followed Miriam out on deck.

"My Bentley is parked in the upper lot. Can I drop you?"

"Yes, near Bayswater. You?"

"Back to Belgravia. There are two or three big parties tonight. I'll change and try to circulate."

"Stay in touch."

"Of course."

EIGHT

Pier 32-B lay on the outer rim of the huge Plymouth Harbor. Pier 32-A was occupied by a Norwegian freighter who was waiting her turn for repairs. Pier 32-C was vacant.

Seaman First Class Ivan Volcek was waved through the checkpoint without anyone bothering to check his ID. Volcek came through every night at the same time, with the same duffel bag over his shoulder.

The old guard at the gate knew what was in the duffel bag: common items bought every day in most any British department store. But they were luxury items—and contraband—in Russia.

It was an unwritten agreement. The Plymouth merchants literally made a killing when a Russian freighter hit port. The seamen would designate one of their own to make the trek ashore and make their purchases.

The officers didn't mind. They had their own designee who went ashore and made *their* purchases.

And everyone made a killing on the black market when they got back home.

Volcek was a big man . . . in fact, *very* big. He stood six-feet-four-inches tall and weighed in at 250 pounds. But by the time he passed under the bow of the freighter moored at Pier 32-B, he was sweating and puffing slightly with the strain of the load.

Along each side of the freighter's bow, barely illuminated by the pier's dim night lights, was the freighter's name and home port. She was the *Volga Tide*, out of one of the principal Soviet Baltic seaports, Tallinn, in the Gulf of Finland.

It was eleven o'clock. In less than a half hour, the *Volga Tide* would cast off and head for home. She would sail through the English Channel into the North Sea. She would make one scheduled stop in Bremerhaven, Germany, before steaming on around Denmark and into the Baltic Sea and home.

As Volcek climbed the gangway, he could already feel the tremors from the big ship's diesels warming up.

Three men met him on the deck and relieved him of the weight.

"Any problem?"

"None. But the old bitch started to weigh a ton after a while. Careful! I don't give a damn about her, but there is good china in there as well."

The four of them carried the duffel bag belowdecks to a cabin reserved for the use of the political officer aboard the ship. When it was opened, they lifted Mildred Hastings out and deposited her unconscious form on a bunk.

"What time do we pick up the other one?"

"Two hours mid-Channel. Shall we tie her?"

"No," Volcek said, "just give her another shot."

He left the cabin and headed for the bridge to inform the captain that their cargo had arrived.

"Davey, 'ere now, keep yer hands to yerself!"

"Y'know you don't mean that," he replied, sliding his hand under the girl's sweater.

"Not in the car, luv. It's so damn uncomfortable, an' besides, someone's liable to see us!"

"Aw, c'mon, luv, who's gonna see us 'ere, huh? We got trees an' bushes all around, an' the river's right there. C'mon, give us a kiss . . ."

The front seat of the car became an explosion of sexuality as the kiss deepened between the young couple. Hands clawed at zippers, tugged at sweaters, and worked on buttons until, suddenly, both of them froze.

"I 'eard somethin'."

"Yeah."

"It's down there, by the river it is . . ."

"There, I see somethin' movin' down there on the jetty!" he hissed, his hands frozen at the clasp of her bra.

It was about fifty yards upstream. A car had glided up to a boat dock with its lights out.

"Yeah, I see 'em! What the devil are they doin'?"

The car's trunk lid was raised and two men were awkwardly pulling a large sack from it. A third person stood nearby, as if overseeing.

"I'd say they's up to no good," the girl whispered.

"Shh, they're goin' out onto the jetty."

Out of the shadow of the boathouse, the trio and their burden could clearly be seen in the moonlight. The young couple both realized at the same time that the third person was a woman. The two men were having quite a struggle with the sack.

They seemed to be discussing something among themselves when they reached the end of the jetty. The woman appeared to be directing the operation.

"Jesus," the girl gasped, "d'you suppose they got a body in that bag?"

"I dunno. Keep quiet!"

There was a sudden movement at the end of the pier and a long shape dropped down to the water. They heard the splash several seconds later, followed shortly by a smaller, quieter splash. The men came back at almost a trot, got in the car from opposite sides, and started the car quietly.

"Can you see the license number?" he said. "Damn, what am I whispering for?"

"I can't . . . there's four or five numbers, I think. Or letters, I can't tell."

"Me, neither." He buttoned up his shirt.

"What are we gonna do?"

"What can we do?" he said. "Shhh!"

The woman was returning to the car now. Just before she reached the shadows of the boathouse, a hand came up to her head. The dark scarf she was wearing was ripped away and she shook out a long, thick mane of black hair. For a few seconds the moonlight gleamed on her face, illuminating it clearly.

Then she was in the car and they were leaving.

"Bloody hell," the boy hissed.

"Whaddaya think we oughta do?"

"Do? . . . Nothin'."

"But shouldn't we tell someone? . . . the coppers?"

"Are you daft, girl? Then yer father'd know, and he'd bloody well want to know what you was doin' down at the river with me!"

"Then you don't think we oughta tell anyone?"

"Damn right I don't," the boy said, running his fingers through his hair. "Jesus, bloody hell, let's get outta here!"

Detective Sergeant Howard Medlin reamed soggy tobacco from the bowl of his pipe and eyed the large round clock on the wall.

He had a half hour until his shift ended.

Medlin always hated holding down the situation desk at Scotland Yard. And he hated it even more on the three-to-midnight shift.

His thoughts were already turning to a bit of a dram and his warm bed, when the jangling telephone broke into his reverie. With a sigh, he reached for the instrument.

"Medlin."

"Cornwall, Sergeant, line three . . . sounds serious."

"Damn," Medlin hissed, and poked the appropriate button. "Detective Sergeant Medlin."

"Edwards here, sir. Chief Constable, Dodman Point."

Medlin knew England like he knew his own bedroom. Dodman Point, just below St. Austell Bay and above Falmouth, near Caerhayes Castle.

"Yes, Edwards, what is it?"

"Bit of a bash down here, I'm afraid. We've got a missing VIP."

"Who?"

"Major General Sir John Hillary."

"Oh, my God."

"Nothing for sure yet, Sergeant, but the wife's in a fluff. Sir John was due home from a bit of fishing at teatime, and he hasn't shown. No real legs on this, but I knew the Yard would know who to inform."

"Dammit, man, he's been missing since teatime and you're just now letting me know? It's near midnight!"

"I know, sir, but you see, Sir John is sometimes late getting home. He's been known to stop at the local pub of an evening and forget to call home."

"Have you checked around?"

"Of course, sir. No one has seen him since this afternoon, and . . ."

"Well?"

"There could be foul play, sir . . . maybe."

"What do you mean, 'maybe'?"

"We found Sir John's hat—his fishing hat—near the south point cove."

"So?"

"According to his wife, Sir John doesn't move without that hat when he's on holiday . . . practically sleeps with the damned thing."

"I'll be right back to you."

Medlin flipped his Rolodex and found the hot number of Home Security.

"Home Office, Nevers."

"Ernie, Medlin at the Yard."

"Yes, Howard?"

"We might have something on that hot sheet you sent over earlier this evening. Just got a call from Cornwall. Sir John Hillary is missing."

"Oh, Lord."

Carter tubed to Paddington Station and walked to the Bayswater section. The farther he went, the smaller the streets became and the grimier the houses.

Even at this late hour, young toughs and even younger tots were in the streets, playing or dealing.

At least eight times in a four-block stretch, he was sized. Carter didn't look like a mug, but he could have been a "face," a member of the underworld fraternity best left alone.

The pub he wanted was on Cropper's Lane. Inside, he ordered a pint of bitter at the bar and carried it to a back booth. Four sneering teen-agers started to shuffle his way. Carter let his coat slide open. At the sight of the shoulder rig, they eased back into their chairs.

Only a hard "face" or a Special Force policeman would carry a concealed piece in London. The boys wanted nothing to do with either of them.

Carter sipped his beer for almost five minutes before he heard the tap of the canes and the clank of the braces. He hardly looked up as Pinky Matthews slid into the opposite side of the booth.

"Hello, Pinky."

"Nick. Long time no see. What brings you down to my patch?"

Carter looked up at last. He had known Pinky Matthews for ten years. The man had looked ancient when Carter first met him. He still did, but the sly cunning in the coal-black eyes never diminished.

"Information."

The old man chuckled. "The last time I gave a copper information, I got these." He hit his legs together under the table. The steel braces made a hollow sound when they collided.

Carter nodded. "I heard about it."

The Killmaster had first met Pinky running guns in Africa. Prior to that, he had been a good second-story man. He should have stayed with it.

A few years before, he had burned an IRA provo cell in Belfast on a shipment of Armalites. To cover his ass, he had turned them in. But MI5 hadn't gotten them all. Two stayed loose and found Pinky.

They hadn't killed him, just kneecapped him with a small-caliber pistol, to set an example.

Now he was back in the fraternity as a small-time fence.

"How's your living, Pinky?"

He shrugged. "Enough for a pint now and then—a woman, when I can occasionally get it up."

"How would you like a warm-weather holiday?"

"Always."

Carter checked the rest of the bar. No one was paying them the slightest attention. He leaned closer to the old man.

"This is outside the fraternity, Pinky. Probably be short employment for a few mugs."

"What's the scam?"

"A snatch, a big one."

"Who?"

"That we don't know. But we think there will be two travelers, both VIP."

Pinky's eyes flinched and it was his turn to scan the bar. When they returned to Carter, they were there and they weren't there.

"There is word on the street. Job's coming down soon. They need two muscles and an ace with his own boat."

"Yeah?"

"The pay is big and it's a short-time shot."

"Anybody bite on it yet?"

"Not that I know of," Pinky replied.

"But you can find out?"

"Maybe."

"A month on Majorca in the sun, with all you can drink and screw."

"Where can I get in touch with you?"

Carter scrawled on a small note pad, tore the sheet out, and passed it across the table. "Either of those numbers can get to me in minutes."

"I'll call you in the morning."

Carter dropped a ten-pound note on the table and stood.

"Take care of yourself, Pinky."

"I'm very careful about that . . . now."

He clanked the braces together again, and Carter left the bar. He was scarcely on the street when the buzzer at his belt went off.

It took him two blocks to find a phone booth that worked.

His call was picked up on the first ring. "Interrupt."

"Carter here."

"Yes, sir. Latest. We think Red Star might have gone active. Major General Sir John Hillary, co-commander NATO Brussels, may have been kidnapped earlier today in south Cornwall."

"But nothing definite?"

"Not yet, sir."

"What about Loring?"

"No contact as yet."

"Anything specifically for me?"

"No, sir."

Carter killed the connection and dialed Miriam Lockwood's Belgravia number. Out of the corner of his eye, he saw three black-leather-jacket types lounging in the nearby darkened doorway.

They were casing him idly with dead eyes.

"Hello?" She sounded out of breath.

"Me. You just got in?"

"Yes, from the parties. I was running for the phone."

"Have you heard? Red Star's active."

"Oh, no."

"Yes. Sir John Hillary. Did you pick up anything to-night?"

"I might have," she replied.

"I'll be there in half an hour. Tell me then."

He hung up and eased the booth door open. The three toughs had moved out of the doorway and now ringed the booth.

Carter didn't feel like fooling around. He kicked the one in the middle in the crotch, then filled his hand with Wilhelmina. Carelessly, he rotated the hot end of the Luger between the other two.

"Pick up your mate and crawl back into your hole."

"You bloody bastard . . ."

Carter jacked a shell into the chamber, and both of them took off in a dead run, leaving their buddy rolling in agony on the sidewalk.

Just no honor among thieves anymore, Carter thought, moving on down the street in search of a cab.

"There they are, two points off the port bow!"

Captain Vladimir Potkinov pulled his pipe from his mouth and squinted his eyes through the thin mist that rolled in hazy waves across the Channel.

Then he saw the flashing light: two shorts, a long, and two more shorts.

"All engines back to one-third. Two points left rudder!"

"Aye, aye, sir."

"Answer the signal."

The order was scarcely given before a light blinked on and off through the fog from the *Volga Tide's* bow. There was another reply from the smaller craft, and Ivan Volcek left the bridge to oversee the docking of the launch.

Captain Potkinov hacked and spit with disgust out of one of the bridge's open portholes.

Damn the KGB, he thought. Potkinov was loyal to Mother Russia, but he was also loyal to the sea and his ship. His ship was his home, and he hated what the KGB did to defile his home.

Ivan Volcek reached the port rail just as the launch eased along the side. There was a whirring sound as the cables dropped from the two arms over the side.

"Secure," came a voice from below. "Haul away!"

The hoist motor engaged and the cables snapped taut. Slowly the launch lifted from the water.

Volcek turned to the two hard-eyed men beside him. Like his own, their faces showed little of the seaman's weathered look. Nor did their hands bear the calluses of a working man of the sea. This was because the three of them had never done manual labor in their lives.

"Everything is ready?"

"Yes, Comrade Volcek."

Both men held silenced pistols at their sides. They were 9mm Makarovs. The 94-grain cartridges in both pistols had been drilled and doctored with a soft lead coating over potassium cyanide.

The short, blond-haired man was the first over the side.

"Greetings, Comrade Major Gorokhov," Volcek said in Russian. "All went well?"

"Without a problem."

Sir John Hillary was handed over the side into three seamen's waiting arms. He was quickly moved back from the rail as the three London "slags" jumped to the deck themselves.

Instantly, they became wary.

" 'Ere now, Izzy, you sod, what's this?"

"Yeah, lad," said the second man. "This 'ere's a bleedin' Russian ship. You didn't say nothin' about truckin' with no Ruskies!"

"Sorry 'bout that, lads," the blond man said in a perfect cockney accent. "But, you see, me name ain't Izzy." Suddenly the cockney was dropped and his speech took on almost perfect Oxbridge diction. "It is Major Illya Vassilovitch Gorokhov,—First Directorate, KGB."

The Makarovs each fired three times. The slugs alone would have done the job, but the cyanide made sure.

"Bag and weight them," Volcek growled, "and dump them when we get back to mid-Channel. Gorokhov, a brandy? We have about five hours before we'll be off St. Abbs Head."

Miriam Lockwood was standing in front of her apartment building when Carter arrived in the taxi.

"They want us at Interrupt right away."

"Get in," Carter said, and turned to the driver. "Oxford Circus."

During the ride, Miriam explained that she had hit three West End parties in rapid succession that evening. The first two bore little or no results, but she might have gotten something at the third.

Abby Sinclair was the fortyish widow of Thomas Sinclair, a rabidly liberal member of Parliament. Since her husband's death, Abby had taken up his convictions with a vengeance.

No one had paid a great deal of attention to her, even after she had joined the People's Party for Peace, and she was often seen around London with Jason Eldridge.

"Who's Jason Eldridge?"

"He is a close business associate of Sir Marcus Loring, and I would imagine one of the movers and shakers in the party."

"I'll dig him out when we get to Interrupt. What about tonight?"

"La Sinclair had quite a bit to drink. She did her usual raving against the Americans and their missiles, and then she said something very odd."

"Like what?"

"Her husband's most powerful enemy in Parliament when he was alive was Mildred Hastings. In fact, Hastings took Sinclair's Devon seat away from him. They hated each other. Tonight, Abby was hinting that she would soon have her revenge on Mildred Hastings. It seems she blames Hastings for the heart attack that took her husband."

"Did she say what form of revenge?"

"No. About that time, Jason Eldridge was able to shut her up."

"Oxford Circus, guv. Which side?"

"This is fine."

Carter paid the cabbie, and they hurried the three blocks to Cavendish Square.

Number 17 was one of those fine old residential buildings that had been built just before World War I and had been partially destroyed during World War II. The government had taken it over in 1947, and in the process of restoring and remodeling it, they had sealed off the top two floors as a private enclave of offices for the intelligence community.

A private elevator in the far rear of the first floor was completely controlled from the top floor. Miriam punched in the correct code numbers, and the elevator door opened. On the fifth floor, the door opened again into a foyer, and their IDs were checked by a plainclothes guard.

When he cleared them, they stepped into the inner sanctum. The room was huge, surrounded by small cubicles, and activity was everywhere. There was little doubt that the whole floor had been taken over for Interrupt command headquarters.

A tall, graying man with a lean, freckled face and tired eyes met them at the door. "Miriam," he said with a slight bow, and turned to the Killmaster. "You must be Carter. I'm Giles Henderson, Special Branch. This way. I'll brief you."

"Giles," Miriam asked as they walked through the room,

"would you have someone check out the whereabouts of Mildred Hastings?"

"Certainly." Suddenly his face got slightly paler. "You have a reason?"

She shrugged. "Just a hunch."

He nodded, and they detoured into one of the cubicles where a young red-headed woman was pounding the keyboard of a computer.

"Joann, hold that for a moment, will you, and give me residences and numbers on Mildred Hastings, M.P. from Devon."

"Certainly."

She cleared the machine, waited until the screen was blank, and began banging away again. Seconds later she ripped off a printout.

"She has a country house in Fareham, a summer flat in Bognor Regis, and her London residence is Mayfair. Here are the numbers."

"I'll take Mayfair," Carter said.

The three of them hit the phones at the same time. Carter waited for twenty rings before he hung up.

"Her nephew is at the summer flat," Miriam said. "He doesn't know where his aunt would be, but he guesses London."

"The housekeeper in Fareham confirms London. She's not expected in the country for at least another fortnight."

"There's no answer in Mayfair," Carter said grimly.

NINE

Carter read the report and then he read it again, down to the last comma. At last he set it down, rubbed his eyes, and sipped at the mug of hot coffee.

Giles Henderson entered the office looking more glum than when he had left to take the call from the Special Branch team that had been sent to Mildred Hastings's apartment.

"Nothing?"

"The super let them in," Henderson offered. "The flat was empty and the bed hadn't been slept in."

"Any signs of a scuffle?"

"None. They found her appointment book. She was to have her hair done at four. They rang up the hairdresser. He says he was there at four and no one answered the bell."

"Has she missed her appointments before?"

"He says no, never."

"Damn," Carter rasped.

"They called up the housekeeper," Miriam said. "A car has been sent for her."

"Looks like we've got other problems, too," Henderson said. "Some news people down in Cornwall have got on to the general's disappearance and put it on the wire. It will probably be all over the television in the morning, as well as the second edition of the papers."

"I just finished the constable's report. They found Sir John's hat, but none of his fishing gear."

"No, and not a trace of it."

"This Garvey Alder . . ."

"Yes, the tea shop owner," Henderson replied. "He saw the general go down to the cove in the afternoon."

"He also mentions seeing a boat, an L-type Royal Navy surplus launch."

"Yes."

"Why would he mention that specifically?"

Henderson smiled. "You're not much of a fisherman, are you, Carter?"

"Not at all."

"The L-type launch is a big, fast, powerful boat. It's designed to move and move fast. At trolling speeds, it's terrible. It would literally shudder. I imagine Alder thought it curious to see two men trolling off its stern."

"I see. My contact mentioned that the word was out on the street for two mugs and an ace who had a boat. Have you checked all the smuggling spots along that coast?"

"Once already, and they're going over it again. We're checking through files now to see who bought that particular L-type boat in the last five years, but I doubt if it will do much good."

"Smuggling?"

Henderson nodded. "They're perfect for it, so they change owners quite often. And sometimes the new owners don't register. Excuse me."

He snatched the ringing phone from its cradle, listened intently, and made a few grunted comments before replacing it.

"The housekeeper says that there are no clothes, other than a pair of dark slacks and a blouse, missing from Mildred Hastings's wardrobe. Also, she has accounted for every piece of luggage the woman owns."

"That does it," Miriam sighed. "Time to round up!"

"Yes," Henderson said. "Several people in Loring's Peace Party have influence, but it's gone beyond that now. We'll round them all up. Excuse me again . . . yes, one second, he's right here."

He handed the phone to Carter and made a hasty exit.

"Carter here."

"You have a call coming in on your private designated number, Mr. Carter. It's a man, and he won't give his name. Shall I switch it over?"

"Yes."

"Go ahead, please."

"Pinky?"

"Yeah, Nick. I put the feet out and a couple of 'em came running back."

"Shoot!"

"It seems a couple of slags are plannin' a long holiday. They've come into quite a spot of money, in dollars. Enough to pay six months ahead in their flat rents."

"Names."

"Paddy Dwyer and Herbie Christie . . . they're both hulks, strictly muscle guys."

"Anything on the ace with the boat?"

"Nil on that, but he probably wouldn't be a London boy anyway."

"Where would I find these two, if they're still around?"

"Paddy lives with a skirt in a fourth-floor walk-up on Farley Hayes Road, right across from Paddington Station. Number Eighteen. Christie's a knockabout, but he keeps a small room in the same building."

"Your voucher's good for Majorca, Pinky. Can you do one thing more?"

"Try."

"The ace may be around somewhere in Cornwall. He sports an L-type launch, Royal Navy surplus."

"Don't know such a bloke, but I might find someone who does."

''Appreciate it.'' Carter hung up and headed for the door. ''Meet you at your place in a couple of hours,'' he murmured to Miriam in passing. ''I might have something.''

Carter cabbed across London to Paddington and walked Praed Street until he found Farley Hayes Road. Number 18 was halfway down a dimly lit block. It was, like all the others on the street, a turn-of-the-century building with a crumbling brick front turned nearly black by the years.

Carter stood across the street, smoking and watching. Eighteen's dirty, tired face seemed to match the faces of the indigent souls who wandered the streets, paying him no mind.

There was the normal amount of foot traffic for the late hour, but no noticeable loiterers like himself. Slowly, he ambled toward the entrance and climbed the steps to a narrow alcove. Along one wall, head high, he found a double row of mailboxes.

P. Dwyer occupied 4-C. If Number 18 followed tradition, that would be the top floor, rear apartment on the right as he faced the building. There was no designation for Herbie Christie, but there was one unmarked box at the end of the row.

Carter picked it. One letter, addressed to H. Christopher-son.

Carter knew that in old buildings such as this, unknown tenant mail with the correct building address went into the super's box, and it usually agreed with a basement bed-sitter.

He went back down the stoop and then down another set of stairs. No designation on the basement door.

He rang the bell four times, with long periods in between. When no sound came from inside, he dug out a penlight and checked the lock: a two-tumbler Humbolt.

It took ten seconds to pick.

Inside was a mess. Whiskey and beer bottles were strewn across the floor, along with partially eaten meals in paper containers and dirty clothing. The furniture consisted of an unmade cot, a few chairs with the stuffing coming out, a single table, and a warm refrigerator.

The fridge had been disconnected. Carter smiled. Even in this chaos, and with his newfound wealth, Herbie Christie had opted to save a few pennies on his power bill.

The only things of interest he found were under the bed: a Cook's Tour brochure of Germany that revealed nothing, and a well-thumbed paperback entitled *Sex In Europe*.

The Killmaster leafed through the paperback and found four pages missing. He flipped back to the index, and identified the chapter title as "Hamburg: Love On the Reeperbahn."

Just in case, he wiped his prints from the book before replacing it. He locked the door behind him and returned to the upper alcove.

The buzz-lock on the front door had long ago given up the ghost. It gave with a solid yank, and Carter padded up the stairs. On the second floor he stepped over an old man cradling an empty gin bottle, and on the third-floor landing an ancient bag lady popped awake at the sound of his tread.

One look at his suit and she knew he didn't belong. "Copper?"

"In a way, Mother, but meanin' no harm to you. D'you know the tenants?"

"A bit," she replied warily.

"Dwyer, Four-C," he said, curling her hand around a ten-pound note.

"Aye," she said, making the note disappear. "Gone the lad is, these two days."

"His skirt?"

"She's there . . . leastways she was earlier this evenin'."

"Would you know her name, Mother?"

"Aye, Libbie, it is. She's a bit of a bitch, givin' me a kick, she does, when she catches me sleepin' on the stairs."

Carter slipped her another bill, a fiver. "Best you find

another place to spend the rest of the night, Mother.''

By the time Carter had reached the fourth-floor landing, the old woman had gone.

He rapped on the door of 4-C. Nothing. He waited ten seconds and rapped again. An ear to the thin panel told him nothing. If Libbie was inside, she made no sound.

There were two locks: one had a keyhole beneath the knob; the other, a newly installed deadbolt in the panel above it.

Carter was just pulling out his picks and a shiv, when there was a whisper from the other side of the door.

Quickly he muffled his mouth with a handkerchief. ''Libbie?''

''Yeah, what is it?''

''Topper's me name, from down Devon way. Got a message from yer lad, I do. He's had a bit of a muck-up.''

He heard the deadbolt roll, and then the door opened on a chain. It barely reached the end of it when her face appeared in the crack and Carter's shoulder hit the door.

The chain pulled out of the wall, and Libbie sailed backward into the room, falling heavily on an ample rump. Carter slammed the door and rolled the deadbolt.

'' 'Ere now, you bloody sod . . .''

She was on her feet and coming at him with the claws of her left hand out and a small wooden stool in her right. She came in swinging the stool with her body tucked, making herself a spare target.

Carter waited until she was only a long step away before he swung his arm in a wide, powerful arc. The flat of his hand caught the side of her face, flat on the cheek.

The blow was calculated, not enough to knock her out or break her jaw, but enough to send her spinning crazily across the room. She hit the wall and started to slide as he reached her.

''You bastard . . .''

Her hand was like a claw as it whipped toward his face. He enveloped it easily in his own fist and squeezed. She screamed. He spun her away from the wall and backhanded the other side of her face. This time the blow was more severe, and the sound of his knuckles against her soft skin was like a shot in the otherwise quiet room.

The back of her knees hit the bed and she landed flat out. To give her credit, she started right back up. He caught her in a half crouch, her legs spread wide, her arms flailing for balance. The fingers of his right hand gripped her throat like a vise, the steel pincer of his thumb over her windpipe.

"Lie down . . . relax," he hissed, his face close enough to hers that tiny flecks of spittle sprayed her frightened eyes. "If you don't, I start with your fingers, then your arms, and finish up with your kneecaps."

Her body went slack and he released her. His own hand shook slightly as he lit a cigarette. She didn't move. She lay on her back, arms and legs spread. Both sides of her face had already started to discolor, taking on a purple to soft red and blue hue where his blows had landed. One eye was clear, the other bloodshot and starting to swell shut.

"Copper?"

"No, lass, collector. Yer Paddy lad owes me mates and me a wee bit of coin. Where's he at?"

"Gone."

"I can see that. Gone where?"

"Frig you."

"Oh, you're a hard'un, ain't you?"

She started off the bed and her face ran right into Carter's hand. He shoved. Her head bounced over off the headboard, and she lay still.

"That's better, lass. You just lay quiet while I do a bit of inventory."

As Carter cased the room, he kept her pinned in the corner of his eye. She was tall, with thick legs and arms that would do credit to a stevedore.

She was not especially pretty. Her bleached hair had long ago given up life, and her face was plain, broad, with a wide mouth. Her nose was too small and her eyes were hard, worried.

The ratty pink robe she wore had fallen open when he shoved her, and she hadn't bothered to gather it. Her breasts were small but still managed to sag, and her behind looked like an extension that was still being built.

"Like what you see, bastard?"

"Not particularly. Goin' somewhere are we, lass?" He hoisted two packed bags.

"To see me mum in the country."

"Is that right?" He spotted her purse on top of the bureau and dropped the bags.

" 'Ere now, leave that be . . ."

He had already dumped the contents. An airline ticket was for the 7:45 A.M. Pan Am from Heathrow to Frankfurt. Inside the folder was also a reservation confirmation for a BMW.

He checked the purse further. The lining came loose. Behind it was a thousand pounds in large bills.

He'd seen enough to drop the act. Taking the wad, he returned to the bed.

"A tidy sum."

" 'Ere now, that's all I got in the world!"

"Was this part of Paddy's down payment on the job?"

Her eyes showed real fear when he switched from cockney into a clearly American accent. "You *are* a copper."

"Not quite. American intelligence working with MI5 and MI6, also Special Branch. You and your boy are in deep trouble, lady."

"Jesus . . ."

"I doubt even he can help you. Who hired Paddy? Who's his contact?"

She looked away, her teeth biting painfully over her split lip. It was the first time her eyes had wavered from his. He could sense the turmoil within her, but he could also guess which side would win.

"We're really not interested in you, Libbie. I want Paddy and who he's doing business with."

"Can I keep the thousand?"

He tossed the pile of notes onto the bed and lit another cigarette. She took it, and still didn't look at him as she spoke.

"Don't know the bloke's name, but there's a number there on the pad by the phone."

Carter tore it off and pocketed it. "Who's the man with the motor launch?"

"Slag, name of Cleaves. That's all I know. Paddy did a dope run with him about a year ago. He's a Weymouth lad."

"Where were you supposed to meet Paddy?"

"Tomorrow . . ." Her eye flickered to the alarm clock. "Tonight, a place outside Hamburg . . . a place called Folgerhaus."

Carter headed for the door. "Take a trip, Libbie. But not to Germany."

"You'll not take me in?"

"Not this time."

"Then there's somethin' else I remember."

"Yeah?"

"The voice on the phone, belongs to that number . . ."

"Yeah?"

"He's a gent, real top hat . . . speech like you hear on the telly."

Carter hit the street, and was frustrated for fifteen minutes finding a cab. It was another twenty before he was checked through into Interrupt.

Giles Henderson was grabbing forty winks on an office cot.

"What's up?"

"Our sailor is named Cleaves. Evidently he works out of Weymouth. Also, check this number out, then get me the sailings of every ship in the last twenty-four hours."

"We had the docks closed off."

"Sure you did, after midnight. What if our ship sailed before then?"

Henderson jumped and Carter headed for the men's room.

He splashed some cold water on his face, fought his hair, and searched for a cup of coffee.

By the time he had stirred sugar into it, a cute computer operator had plopped a stack of computer printouts in front of him.

Twenty minutes later, Henderson returned. "The number belongs to a call box in Bloomsbury."

"It figures," Carter growled. "What about our Weymouth boy?"

"Cleaves, Charles A., a.k.a. Choddy. Nicked five times, only two big. Strong-arm robbery, got five, did three. Last time running dope, did six of a ten in Dartmoor. Got out a little over a year ago. He and his brother run a commercial fishing operation in Weymouth. It's the brother who's listed as the owner of the L-type launch."

"Pick him up if he's around. My guess is he isn't."

"A team's on the way."

"Good. I think I found a winner. The *Volga Tide*, home port Tallinn. Sailed last night from Plymouth at eleven thirty-three. Cleared the harbor master at eleven fifty-five. Destination, home port."

"Dear God, they wouldn't stow two U.K. VIPs aboard a Russian freighter!"

"They might, if they could get rid of them. The *Volga Tide* has a one-night layover in Bremerhaven, Germany."

"You think they'll dump them there?"

"If they don't get them off at sea. Have you got anything in the North Sea . . . about here . . . that can intercept and watch them into Bremerhaven?"

"This way!"

They entered one of the computer cubicles where the same young woman who had delivered the printout to Carter was sipping coffee. Henderson told her what they needed in short, terse sentences.

"Yes, we have a Corsair there, H.M.S. *Dauntless*. Skipper is Commander Higgins."

"I'll get on the radio to him right away."

Henderson scooted from the room and the woman answered the phone. "It's for Mr. Henderson."

"I'll take it. Carter here."

"Don't know you, but I suppose you're with Special Branch."

"Attached. Who is this?"

"Medlin, Scotland Yard. My lads have identified a body a tour boat fished out of the Thames. It's Sir Marcus Loring."

"What have you got?"

"Shot once in the head, died instantly. Medicos put it about twelve hours ago. He was weighted down, but the line holding the weights came apart. He came up near the Lots Road power station, below Battersea Bridge. The widow is identifying now."

"Any chance of keeping it out of the papers?"

"None. They're already on to it."

"Damn," Carter breathed.

"Obstacles of a free society."

"Thanks, Medlin. I'll pass it along."

"Righto."

Henderson was at his elbow. "Loring's dead. He was dumped in the Thames."

"All right, we'll squeeze Jason Eldridge and the Sinclair woman a little harder. God, we're going to have a lot of VIPs pissed off."

"Name of the game," Carter said. "What have you got for me?"

"Foreign Office has a Copeland eight-passenger twin-jet at its disposal out of Gatwick. Captain R.A. Garfield. Fog's in. They figure it will lift around eight, maybe eight-thirty."

"Okay," Carter sighed. "Call me at Miriam's when it does. I'm going to crash until then."

"Will do."

Henderson had a car and driver waiting for him at the stoop. Miriam met him at the door.

''You look like hell.''

''I feel worse.''

He brought her up to date as he stripped out of his clothes on the way to the bedroom.

''We head for Germany as soon as the fog lifts. What time is it?''

''Four.''

''Jesus.''

He was asleep almost as soon as his head found the pillow.

Ten seconds later, he heard a female voice whispering his name. The voice sounded as though it were rising slowly from a well.

It finally awakened him.

It was several seconds after his eyes opened that he got his bearings. Miriam stood, half dressed, at the foot of the bed, pulling a dark sweater over her head.

''The call just came,'' she murmured.

''What time is it?''

''Eight.''

''My God,'' he groaned, rolling out of the bed.

''They have a driver on the way. A helicopter is coming down from Northolt to take us to Gatwick. He'll land on the Hyde Park pad.''

''Good,'' Carter said, stumbling toward the shower.

''I have some rolls buttered and coffee made.''

''Put it all in a thermos and doggie bag. Let's get the hell out of here.''

TEN

They landed at Kablehoffen, a private strip at the halfway point between Bremerhaven and Hamburg. Both of the West German counterintelligence agencies, the *Militärischer Abschirmdienst* and the *Bundesamt fur Verfassungsschutz,* had been alerted to their arrival.

The plane had just settled into its chocks when two leather-coated men emerged from a black Mercedes and walked toward it through a light rain.

"Herr Carter, Fräulein Lockwood?"

They both nodded and produced IDs. The two Germans did likewise.

"I am Heinrich Keller, M.A.D. My colleague with the B.f.V., Peter Reinbold."

"Gentlemen," Carter nodded. "Can we get started?"

"Of course."

They moved quickly through the drizzle to the car. Keller gave the driver orders, and moments later they had left the airfield. Once they were on the highway toward Bremerhaven, Carter started his questions.

"Have you been in touch with the *Dauntless* and Commander Higgins?"

"We have," Reinbold answered, struggling a North Sea map across their laps. "The *Volga Tide* is right on its sailing schedule. The *Dauntless* picked it up just off the northern coast of the Netherlands . . . here."

"What's their present position?"

"Just off the Ostfriesische Islands . . . here, above Norderney."

"And so far there hasn't been a break in the speed, or a smaller craft leaving the ship?" Miriam asked.

"None. This rain won't help, but as you know, the *Dauntless* has the latest in radar. If even a swimmer left the *Volga Tide*, Commander Higgins would know it."

"What's their ETA in Bremerhaven?" Carter asked.

"Six fifty-five in the strait, docking at seven-forty. We've already contacted the *Volga Tide* and passed docking instructions. We've given them an isolated pier so there will be less notice taken of the impounding and search."

Carter nodded. "You haven't notified the Soviet legation in Hamburg?"

Reinbold smiled. "It's been in the works for an hour, but we've had tremendous paper foul-ups. Chances are they won't be informed until around seven-thirty."

By that time, Carter thought, the *Volga Tide* would be swarming with German security and customs agents.

"How about your locals in the People's Party for Peace?"

Both Keller and Reinbold displayed sour faces. The latter extracted a list from his inside pocket and consulted it.

"There are four leaders around the country. We have had all of them under constant surveillance since yesterday morning. They seem to be moving, but, as yet, not in any definite direction."

Carter checked his watch. It was nearly noon, several hours before they could search the *Volga Tide*.

When Miriam suggested lunch, he readily agreed.

After a light breakfast, Norman Dufont emerged from the

Bloomsbury flat and walked the short distance to Chubb's underground garage. He passed over his parking ticket and moments later took over a deep-green Jaguar sedan.

The traffic was light on the M1 north, and he was able to reach the Harrow cutoff in less than an hour.

He wound through the old section, past Harrow School, and came out on a flat plain literally polka-dotted with new development. The clutch of small new houses he sought was called The Dells. When he spotted the sign, he drove into the development and found Dellmar Close.

Number 12 was four houses from the cul-de-sac. He touched the automatic door opener when he hit the drive, and coasted the Jaguar into the garage.

A door opened directly into the kitchen. He smelled fresh coffee, spotted the pot, and poured himself a cup.

He could hear her footsteps coming from the other end of the house.

"It's me, my dear. Any word of their arrival yet?"

"None," came the reply, and then she stepped into the kitchen.

Dufont turned to face her. "Ah, lovely as usual."

She was about thirty, with black hair, silky, unpowdered skin, and a lush but well-shaped mouth without lipstick that looked willful in repose and mischievous in smiles. She wore gold coins for earrings, and her dark eyes looked out between blackened lashes. Her tongue had a fetching trick of darting out to moisten her lips. Her yellow print dress was fashionable, but with her figure and her dancer's grace of movement, she could make a rag look chic.

"Bad show that, the body surfacing so soon."

She nodded. "If we could have more illegals and not have to depend on local sympathizers, mistakes like that wouldn't happen."

"How did it go at headquarters?"

"Not bad," she said and shrugged. "I made the identification, did a little weeping."

"Questions?"

"Of course. I pleaded innocent to most of the People's Party business. They seemed to accept it."

"Let's hope they do. It will be imperative."

She freshened the cup in her own hand. "There was a great blurb on the telly this morning about Sir John, but nothing about Mildred Hastings."

"I know," Dufont replied, sipping from his cup. "My guess is that MI5 and Special Branch are well aware of our brilliant Conservative M.P.'s disappearance, as well as Hillary's. They have just managed to keep it from the news people."

"Rotten luck, the business with Pierre Delamaine."

"Yes, it is, but it might be to our advantage and give you more time. Do you have your equipment ready?"

"Of course. I told my solicitor and the maid that I couldn't stand London or the media pressure. I had to get away, by myself."

"Understandable. Do you think they bought it?"

"Why shouldn't they?"

Dufont shrugged and washed out his cup. "No reason, really. Let's be on our way, shall we? We can ring up our keepers from a rest stop on the motorway."

"I'll put on my Abby Sinclair wig."

She turned and walked from the room, and Dufont throught how delightfully erotic she made the simplest move. But then that was what she had been trained to do her whole life: entice.

Of course she had other attributes and functions. She was also trained to do marvelous things with needles, and to calibrate the information her needles obtained.

Her code name was Carla. Her real name was Gerta Hessling. And for the last three years, she had been Lady Phyllis Loring.

Presently she was a widow.

● ● ●

"Pardon me fer bustin' in, missus, but I've got to see Davey!"

"He's upstairs in his room, Jenny. What is it?"

"Somethin' very important. I'll find the way."

" 'Ere now, you can't just go bustin' into the lad's room. It ain't proper, it ain't—"

But the young girl had already run up the stairs and begun rapping on the closed bedroom door. "Davey, Davey, it's me, Jenny!"

She didn't wait for a reply but opened the door, popped in, and quickly closed it behind her.

" 'Ere, Jenny, are you daft?" The boy was just pulling on a pair of jeans over his naked body. "Me mum's right downstairs!"

"Forget yer mum. Have you seen the mornin' papers?"

"Nah. Had a bit of a tiddle with the lads after I dropped you off last night. Just gettin' up now."

"Look at this!"

She thrust a newspaper into his hand and stabbed a finger at a front-page picture. The boy scowled at the fuzzy, dark image of a well-dressed woman leaving a building with an official-looking man on each arm.

"So what?" Suddenly his teeth clamped into his lower lip and the blood drained from his face, leaving it ashen. "B'Jesus, it's her—the woman at the river!"

"You're bloody right it is! And the bloke she just identified is her own husband, Sir Marcus Loring."

"Go on with you!"

"It is! Read the story!"

His eyes scanned down the article: Wife Identifies Husband's Body Dragged from Thames.

"See?"

"The bloody witch," he choked. "She tossed his arse into the river, then goes to the coppers to identify him."

"You know what we gotta do, Davey."

Suddenly the boy's mother barged through the door, fury on her face.

" 'Ere, what we got goin' 'ere? And you, Davey, wi' half yer duds on! Get down to the sittin' room, the both of you, like decent folk."

"Mum?"

"Aye?"

"Shut up an' get out. Jenny an' me, we got to talk."

Carter's feet squished soddenly in his shoes as he shifted his weight from foot to foot. The overhang and the umbrella he held did little to stop the falling rain from finding its way down the back of his neck.

He could have waited in the harbor master's office, but he was too nervous. A hundred yards in front of him at Pier 3-Blue, lights blazed on every deck of the *Volga Tide*, and he could see men moving over her like bees on a honeycomb.

They had been at it for nearly three hours now, and as each minute wore on, the chances for success looked dimmer and dimmer.

Even as this thought pounded at the back of his weary eyes, Carter saw the dark-coated figures of Keller and Reinbold walk down the bow gangway and head for the harbor master's office.

He shook himself into action and headed in the same direction, beating them to the office by about a minute. The looks on their wide, Teutonic faces told him as much as their quick verbal reports.

"You're sure?" Carter said, feeling the rain turn to sweat in the small of his back.

"Positive," Reinbold said, his hard dark eyes burning with the same rabid intensity the Killmaster felt. "We used two sixteen-man crews and we took her apart from stem to stern, everything but tear the bulkheads off."

"Damn," Carter hissed.

"There's not a Brit on board . . . man, woman, or child."

"And the crew manifest checked?"

"Down to a man," Reinbold growled, then cursed in German. "The captain is filing a formal protest with Bonn right now. If we push them much further, we'll be in up to our ass."

Carter ground out his cigarette and turned to Commander Arnold Higgins. He was a big, solid man with calm eyes, a full head of gray hair, and twenty-two years of naval service. The *Dauntless* had dropped anchor center harbor an hour before, and its skipper had coptered in to join them.

"Commander, was there any chance they could have gotten off?"

"I hardly think so . . . no, I'm positive of it."

"Even with the fog and the rain?"

"No way. The *Dauntless* is equipped with every new-fangled gear known to science. I even logged when they threw their garbage over."

Carter cursed again and seized a chart of the North Sea. "Show me exactly where you picked them up."

"Right here, off Aberdeen."

Carter turned back to Reinbold. "And there was no L-type launch stowed away or on the hoisting cranes?"

"The only boats on any of the hoisting cranes were old-fashioned outboard-powered Soviet lifeboats."

"It doesn't figure," Carter whispered. "The general had to be taken out by sea. Every small craft coming into Plymouth went through the harbor master, and there wasn't a single one of that class."

"If you'll pardon me," Higgins said. "They couldn't have put a boat off in the Channel between Dover and Calais. There's too much traffic in there; they would have been monitored. Their last checkpoint was Sunderland, here, before Aberdeen."

"Where you picked them up?"

"That's correct."

"So they could have put ashore somewhere between Sunderland and their Aberdeen weather check?"

"That's right."

"Over four hundred miles of irregular coastline. It would be like finding a tick on a two-hundred-pound hound dog."

"Begging your pardon, sir," Higgins offered, "but you said military maritime was tracing down that L-type launch. It might be a long shot, but Scotland Yard could have the locals all along here check every boat slip."

Carter nodded. "It will take time, but it's better than nothing. Miriam, will you see to it?"

"I'll get right on to London." She slipped from the room as a junior German officer entered and pulled Keller to the side.

"Commander," Carter continued, "could they have gone this way, toward the Belgian or French coast?"

"They could have, but from the spotting track we made of the *Volga Tide's* sailing path, it would be highly unlikely and uselessly dangerous. The sea got a bit high out there tonight. The distance to the French or Belgian coast would be three times what it was to Scotland."

"Herr Carter . . ."

It was Keller at his elbow. "Yes?"

"Our four People's Party patriots have come to ground."

"Where?"

"A hunting lodge near Bad Zwischenahn."

Carter dove for a map. Keller quickly pinpointed the locale.

"A straight shot from Bremerhaven, just up from Oldenburg."

Keller nodded. "It's isolated and private. My men have roused merchants in the area. They've made several food deliveries to a hunting lodge here in the last few days."

"Preparing for a long stay . . ."

"It would seem so."

"Your people have it under surveillance?" Carter asked.

"They do—a four-man team."

"What do you think?" Carter said.

"No disrespect to Commander Higgins, but if they did manage to get off the *Volga Tide*, that would be a perfect place to keep the hostages."

Carter leaned over the map, his mind racing. He sincerely believed that the skipper of the *Dauntless* was right. If they took the two VIPs off the *Volga Tide*, it was probably to Scotland before the Corsair was able to pick them up.

But it was all a guessing game, and Carter couldn't afford to guess wrong.

"What standard of team are your men down there?"

Keller smiled. "They're from Strategic—top flight, all of them."

Carter sighed. "All right, let's take them and see what we've got."

It was nearly midnight by the time Dufont turned off the M1 at Newcastle upon Tyne and bore inland on 696.

He had stopped a half hour before at an all-night truckers' restaurant on the outskirts of Sunderland to make the call.

It was picked up on the third ring with no vocal answer. This was what Dufont had expected.

"The moon was very bright over the Channel tonight," he said.

"Not bright enough to illuminate the passage of the hawks," came the reply.

Dufont had expected no trouble, but nevertheless the correct reply made him sigh with relief.

"I assume all went well?"

"They are still sleeping peacefully. We are four at the house."

"And your arrival caused no stir in the populace?"

"None. You are close by?"

"A little more than an hour. I'll see you then."

Dufont rounded a curve, and when his headlights picked up a long, straight stretch of road, he pushed the powerful car up to eighty.

Sir Marcus Loring's widow stirred in the passenger seat.

"How much farther?" she asked.

"A half hour to the Bellingham turnoff, and then maybe fifteen minutes to the estate."

"Sorry I slept all the way."

"Don't worry about it," Dufont replied. "It's you who will have to do all the work when we arrive."

"I just hope I can get everything in thirty-six hours."

"The funeral?"

"Yes," she nodded. "Ten in the morning, day after to-morrow."

"How long will you be forced to play the grieving widow?"

She chuckled. "Just until the shock wears off and my tender sensibilities can be soothed by time."

In the warmth of the car, Norman Dufont suppressed a shudder. He knew that the woman beside him had no sensibilities.

"Here we are."

The car's powerful headlight beams pierced the narrow asphalt road as it climbed through overhanging tree branches. It wound and twisted for nearly a mile before it became a narrower, single, graveled lane.

"How did you find this place?"

"It belongs to an old hunting chum of mine, Sir Walter Hedgeman. He's vacationing in the south of France for a month. He was only too happy to lend me its use. Especially when I told him I needed it for an affair of the heart with a married woman."

Dufont slowed as they rode between fieldstone walls and white, estate-type fences. At last, through the bars of a tall, wrought-iron gate, they saw lights emanating from the windows of a white brick Georgian manor.

He signaled with his lights, and the gate swung smoothly open. The Jag moved through and the gates closed silently behind it.

"No guard?"

"None needed. The whole estate is lined with trip wires and electronic eyes. Both gates have infrared cameras monitored from the house. It's all infinitely more reliable than the human eye. Sir Walter is very security conscious."

"Servants?"

"Also on holiday."

"You're very thorough, Norman."

"I know."

Meticulous lawns spread outward like a lush green fan from the house, and wrought-iron lamps made little pools of light around the U-shaped drive. Dufont parked under a vaulted porte cochere, and together they mounted the steps toward the open door.

"Volcek?"

"Yes, comrade. And this is Major Gorokhov."

"Good to meet you both." Dufont did not introduce Carla. Her identity was only on a need-to-know basis, and these two men didn't need to know. "Where are they?"

"In the library. We have rigged the billiard table and a large sofa as you requested."

"Good. Lead the way." The two KGB officers moved down a long, wood-paneled hall, with Dufont and Carla right behind them. She was already working the clasps of the bag she carried. "The gentlemen from London?"

"In the Channel."

"Excellent. And the boat?"

"Scuttled about two hundred yards off St. Abbs Head. We bound the fisherman's body to it before it went down."

Dufont nodded with satisfaction. No trace. The cleaners in London could identify him, but they wouldn't dare. Their own implication was too deep and too long. They would only be frying in their own fat.

"Here we are."

Twin mahogany doors were pushed open and they entered a large, book-lined room.

The house thus far was almost baronial in its architecture and decor, with dark ceiling beams and darkly paneled walls. This study was no different.

Light was provided by two massive chandeliers and several lamps. Without a word, Carla went about repositioning the lamps so that they provided a more muted illumination. As she killed the overhead lights, she nodded at Dufont.

"We won't be needing you gentlemen in attendance," he said.

Without a word of argument, the two KGB officers slipped from the room. Dufont locked the door behind them and turned to find Carla already meticulously unpacking the instruments from her bag and laying them out in a provided space.

"You are familiar with the tape equipment?" she asked.

"Of course."

She nodded, filling a hypodermic from a glassine packet. The nod was a command. Dufont moved into the area behind the tape recorders, and began activating and checking the equipment.

Sir John Hillary lay on a mattress on the billiard table. Carla would start with him.

She checked his pupils, his pulse, and his respiration.

"Start the equipment."

Dufont did.

Carefully she injected Sir John and sat back to wait, timing his reactions with a stopwatch hung around her neck.

"He's ready."

"The tape is running."

Once again she checked the man's pulse, and then dabbed at his brow with a damp cloth.

"General . . . General?"

"Yes," came the whispered response.

"This is Captain Anderson, General . . . your secretary, Captain Nella Anderson."

"Yes, Nella."

"RHQ, NATO London, and NORDAC Washington want us to review the recent arrivals, General."

"Very well."

"We'll start with London, Sheffield section. Is that all right?"

"Of course."

"Very well. If you will relay, then, the number of missiles in the Sheffield area—their nuclear strength, their range, their deployment, and their time of activation, both offensively and defensively, against enemy strike time."

"Of course," answered the man on the table. "Of course. Sheffield, designated D-12 . . . made up of NATO quadrants 27, 29, 31, and 33. Nine ICBMs, all with dummy warheads."

"Very good, General."

"Thank you, Nella. Throat's bloody dry. Could I have a glass of water, please?"

"Of course." Gently she lifted his head and put the glass to his lips.

"Did you send the flowers to Gladys for our anniversary?"

"Yes, I did, General."

"Thank you, Nella. The old girl loves a posy now and then, you know."

"I know, General. Shall we continue?"

"By all means."

"Good. Cheviot Hills section . . . southern Scotland."

"Cheviot Hills . . . designated D-11, made up of NATO quadrants 13, 15, and 17. Six long-range Baleric missiles with one-megaton warheads . . . active . . ."

As Sir John's voice droned on, the man and the woman exchanged broad smiles.

The general's mind was everything his deep file maintained it was.

The man had a photographic memory.

ELEVEN

Keller drove, with Reinbold in the passenger seat and Miriam and Carter in the rear. Word had already been sent to the team at the hunting lodge. Everything would be in readiness when they arrived.

Like a big, purring cat, the Mercedes left the main road and moved stealthily through the thick forest. One of the rear windows was cracked a bit and the night air wafted around Carter's face, clearing his thoughts.

He didn't expect any huge results from the night raid, but at least they might find another piece of the puzzle.

They entered and left the small village without seeing a soul. That was good.

About a mile beyond the village, Keller pulled over and parked. He blinked his lights, and got an answering flash from deep in the woods.

"That will be Hans on the perimeter. We'll walk from here."

The three men shared the radio equipment, and they set off. Another mile, and a second flash took them off the narrow, graveled road. Minutes later they entered a clearing.

Carter and Miriam were brusquely introduced to the leader

of the team, Hans Freitog. He was a hulking bear of a man, with shaggy black hair, dead eyes, and deep scars on both sides of his face. He fit the profile of a thousand such men Carter had met or known in the service around the world.

They met in the center of the clearing. The three men around Freitog all looked at the world with the same eyes. Pistols were stuck in their belts and, to a man, they sported more powerful artillery on their shoulders.

There was no handshake and only a bare vocal greeting before they got down to business. They spoke German.

"There are three men and one woman in the lodge. They arrived separately, one with radio equipment, but as yet they have not used it. We have already tapped the telephone line into the house. They made one call, to Hamburg."

"And . . . ?" Carter asked.

"There was no answer. There are three entrances: front, back, and a cellar door. The cellar seems to be for wine and does not appear to have inside access."

Throughout the explanation, Carter had been nodding. Now he motioned toward the weapons each of the men carried.

"The ammunition you have been issued will do the job?"

Hans gestured, and one of the men passed him a stubby gun that looked like a bazooka.

"We all have stun guns. Two of my men will be backup with rubber bullets."

"And if they are heavily armed and retaliate?" Carter asked.

Keller replied, "Then we must step in with live ammunition."

"I understand," Carter said.

Hans continued. He ejected a bulky shell from the odd weapon in his hand and held it up to the AXE agent.

"The casing is normal. The shell itself is only a thin veneer. Inside it is another shell containing gas. The charge for the projectile is less because of the shell's diminished weight. Therefore the velocity is less. We'll have to be very close to have ultimate accuracy through the windows, but the chance for loss of life is almost nil.''

"Good," Carter said, and turned to Miriam. "You'll handle communications. We must all know each other's locations at all times.''

"Of course," she replied, nodding, and went to work unpacking the equipment.

Carter again addressed the men. "There are seven of us. Keller and Reinbold will take the backup, with live ammunition. Let's hope they won't be needed. Hans, you take your gas men to the rear with Keller. I'll handle the front with the other three.''

There were a few vocal affirmative replies and they were all nodding. These were hard men, used to doing what they were told, no matter what it was.

Carter knew they would do this job like any other.

"Miriam?''

"Ready.''

They all shrugged into the harnesses holding the light-weight, battery-powered sets, and adjusted the headsets to their ears and the wire-mike in front of their lips.

"Voice check," Miriam said.

As each of them came in loud and clear to Miriam and the others, she nodded and adjusted levels.

"Ready.''

"All right," Carter said, "let's go. Hans, we'll give you ten minutes to get around to the rear.''

Keller, Freitog, and one of his team moved off through the trees. Carter checked the luminous dial of his watch, and then the sky. A quarter moon and lots of stars. The forest around them was greenly cool, and smelled of pine resin and decaying wood.

All in all, it was a beautiful evening. The Killmaster hoped it would stay that way.

He licked his lips. He wanted a cigarette but pushed the thought from his mind.

"Here . . . and set up.''

"Let's go," Carter said without looking at Reinbold or the other two men.

They fanned out through the trees, the man carrying the gas gun in the point. Suddenly he froze in his tracks.

"What is it?" Carter whispered.

"Trip wire . . . there, six inches off the ground. And there's another about five feet farther on."

"Hans, you hear that?"

"*Ja.* We'll watch ourselves back here!"

Carefully, they stepped high over the trip wires and advanced again. Fifty yards from the lodge, they paused and hunkered down.

The lodge contained two floors. It was an A-frame, with just one large room and probably a kitchen. The bedrooms would be ringed on the upper level around a walkway.

Lights blazed in the main room, and a single bulb gleamed behind a shuttered window in the upstairs.

"Freitog?"

"*Ja?*"

"Looks like we got one awake upstairs."

"*Ja.* I'm sending my man forward with the gas pistol."

"Me, too," Carter replied, and nodded at his own point man.

The man moved forward without a sound or a faltering step. Eyes like a cat, Carter thought.

"In place," came the voice from the rear.

"Same here," whispered Carter's man.

"Fire!" Carter hissed.

The explosions came one upon the other. By the time the man had reloaded and another explosion burst into the night, Carter and the second man were at the door.

"Do it!" Carter growled.

The bull gun in the man's hand exploded twice, a shell each for the door's hinges. It sagged, and Carter hit it with his shoulders.

A man and a woman were already reeling from the gas as

Carter rolled into the room and brought up the stun pistol in both hands.

A second man was lurching toward the rear door.

Carter fired and missed.

He heard his backup hit the floor beside him as the man yanked the rear door open.

"Coming your way, Hans!"

"Got him!"

The words had scarcely left his mouth when the runner screamed and staggered back into the room holding his chest. He'd been hit with a rubber bullet.

"Carter, the landing!"

The Killmaster looked up through the gray haze of the rising gas. A man stood on the balcony, sighting down the barrel of a shotgun.

Carter rolled just as flame erupted twice in rapid succession from the barrels.

He heard a scream and saw the semiconscious man on the floor clutch one of his legs. The one on the balcony started reeling as the gas rose to his level, but he was sighting the shotgun again, this time on the woman.

"Reinbold!" Carter barked.

"Got him!"

The words were barely out when the powerful Mauser in Reinbold's hand cracked twice.

The shotgun clattered from the man's hands and thudded on the floor below. He clutched his gut, tottered, and then crashed through the railing to join it.

Carter was on him in seconds, the stun gun pressed to his neck.

There was no need. The man was dead.

"Sorry," Reinbold said.

"Couldn't be helped," Carter replied. "See to the wounded man. Hans . . . Keller!"

"*Ja.*"

"Here."

"It's done. One of theirs is dead, and one wounded. No hits on our side. We set up interrogation as soon as the gas dissipates."

He helped get the wounded man outside into the clean air. Some of the buckshot had creased his right leg. It wasn't serious.

Through the open door he could see Hans and his men already injecting the live man and woman on the floor. With any luck, the antidote to the gas would take effect right away.

They should be alert enough for interrogation in less than an hour.

Carla finished splashing cold water on her face and reached for a towel. As she stepped away from the washbasin, Norman Dufont took her place.

Through the windows of the adjacent bedroom, dawn was just starting to break.

Dufont followed her into the bedroom. "Do you want to rest awhile before we start again?"

"No," she said and smiled, "the adrenaline's still pumping. It's not taking nearly as long as we planned."

"His memory is phenomenal."

"I know. We'll give him some rest and start on the woman. Let us hope the information we have on her is equally as correct."

"I'm sure it is."

The two of them returned to the study on the main floor. The woman carefully inserted an IV in Sir John Hillary's arm and adjusted the drip of the glucose solution.

When she was satisfied, she turned her attention to Mildred Hastings. The woman was starting to stir as the original sleep-inducing solution wore off. That was good.

Another needle was prepared and the solution containing powder from a glassine envelope was injected into the M.P. from Devon's arm.

Carla checked the stopwatch around her neck, then looked

at Dufont. "It will take about twenty minutes. Turn the tape deck on."

Dufont flipped a switch. There was a slight hum, and then the voice of the prime minister of England came from the twin speakers. From her tone, the tenor, and the content of her speech, she was obviously addressing Parliament.

She let the tape play for a good ten minutes, then signaled Dufont to shut it off. As he removed that tape and replaced it with a blank one that would eventually record Mildred Hastings's conversation, Carla closed her eyes and concentrated on the voice she had just heard.

"Want to try it?" Dufont murmured.

She nodded, took a deep breath, and began to speak. "Ladies and gentlemen of Parliament, I have come to address you today on matters of grave importance to us all . . ."

For a full three minutes, she spoke extemporaneously in the voice of the prime minister of England. When she halted at last, she turned to Dufont. He was smiling and shaking his head in obvious admiration.

"Perfect."

"Pour us a cuppa then, and we'll begin."

Two cups of tea were poured. When cream and sugar had been added and Dufont had returned to his equipment, Carla moved to a chair beside Mildred Hastings.

"Mildred . . . Mildred . . . can you hear me?"

"Yes."

"How do you feel, Mildred?"

"Fine. A little drowsy, but fine."

"I'm so glad you could join me this evening for a little chat, Mildred."

"It's no trouble at all, Madame Prime Minister. I am only too happy to drop by."

"Good, thank you. Now, if you don't mind, we'll get right to the reason I asked to see you."

"Of course."

"Good. Now, the Americans have been pressing me for our results on Operation Overland. You've seen the reports from the foreign secretary and our people at MI6?"

"Yes, I have. The operation is proceeding beyond our wildest dreams. We have managed to set up at least one deep-cover operative in each of the Eastern satellite internal security services."

Dufont and Carla exchanged shocked glances. He motioned her to continue.

"Can you reiterate, Mildred, the importance of this?"

"Of course. By having a highly placed operative in each of these services, we will know the comings and goings of all Soviet and satellite agents to the West, as well as advance warning when any of our own agents are about to be blown."

"I'm very pleased, Mildred, very pleased."

"Thank you."

"Of course, I would like to know the caliber of information we can get from these people. I assume they are placed very high?"

"Very high," Mildred Hastings replied.

"Shall we start with Hungary?"

"Of course. Hungary. Jan Potemchik. He is the second chairman in charge of liaison with Moscow, with access to GRU and KGB files on all known agents in his country or passing through to the West. He has also been able to move two of our people into his department, and . . ."

As Mildred Hastings recited from the well of her phenomenal memory, Carla began to perspire. When she glanced at Norman Dufont, his face was ashen.

Neither of them had any idea that Operation Overland had gone so far.

The puzzle was the fact that three of them were unarmed and practically laid down, while one of them grabbed a shotgun and started blasting away.

It was solved by piecing together what the other three said about number four.

He was down as Helgar Erikson, a Swede, born in Stockholm, involved in trade with a couple of German companies. After a little prying, it came out that his real name was Helmut Eindbaden. Miriam was on the radio with an open scramble channel to Bonn. One time through the M.A.D. computers with that name, and it didn't take long.

"He's with East German foreign intelligence, a propaganda officer and organizer. He specializes in student unrest, demonstrations, the rest."

"That would explain it. He was their control, at least in Germany. Let's dig."

They dropped Eindbaden and went to work on the other three.

The two men were Wolfgang Walther and Karl Von Leissling.

Walther was the scion of a wealthy chemical manufacturing family, and had long been associated with a multitude of left-wing causes. He had joined the People's Party two years earlier and had risen to be a sector leader.

Von Leissling's background was about the same, with the same advancement. His main claim to fame was being a Bavarian playboy, and he had been associated with a few terrorist groups but was never trusted with any work that was serious.

The biggest break came when they got down to brass tacks with the woman. Her name was Roberta Kirsch. She was twenty-two years old and had been a college dropout for the past two years. Her recruitment had been out of a small group called the Coalition for a Nuclear-Free Germany. She was still a salaried organizer for that group, but for the past two years she had also been deeply involved with the People's Party.

Keller and Reinbold took turns working on her over a two-hour period. A pair of stenos had been brought in, so typed pages of the interrogation were passed to Miriam and Carter practically out of her lips.

Yes, she knew that two very important, prowar, pronuclear imperialists were to be kidnapped and detained. The reason? To tell the world that lovers of peace were no longer going to stand by while American warmongers planted their instruments of death on European soil.

No, she didn't know what the ransom demands were to be. She didn't need to know to carry out her part of the objective.

The group's instructions were to assemble in the lodge and wait for the delivery of the two VIPs. Once that was done, they were to watch over them until the party's demands were met.

Then what?

Then they were to be reinjected, and a phone call would be made to the authorities, informing them where the couple could be picked up.

The interrogation went on like this until dawn started seeping over the horizon.

Keller and Reinbold joined Miriam and Carter for coffee.

"She's the idealist of the group," Carter commented.

Keller nodded. "No doubt about it, hard-core, steeped up to here with the rhetoric."

"But she looks upon herself as a true patriot," Miriam said.

"They all do," Reinbold offered. "And they love to tell you so."

Carter rose with a sigh. "I'd like to try a little tack of my own, do you mind?"

Keller shrugged his shoulders wearily.

"If you're going to slap her around," Reinbold added, "do it where it doesn't show. We have very little to charge them with as it is."

Carter poured two cups of coffee and walked into the other room. She sat stiffly on the edge of a chair, probably exactly as Reinbold and Keller had left her.

"Coffee?"

"Thank you."

"Cigarette?"

"I don't smoke."

"Mind if I do?"

"They are your lungs."

Carter lit up and cased her through the smoke.

She was a skinny, long-legged girl who probably galloped instead of walked. Her face was very white, with a small, pinched mouth and a sharp chin. Her hair was mousy brown over intense blue eyes, her best feature.

Her clothing consisted of a tight skirt, heavy mesh stockings, boots, and a black plastic-trying-to-be-leather jacket.

"My name is Carter. I'm an American."

"Really? Your German is excellent."

"I don't like nuclear bombs either."

"Then you should join us instead of harassing us."

"But I also don't believe in kidnapping."

Silence.

"You knew, of course, that Helmut Eindbaden was an East German agent."

"I didn't know. I suspected. As long as he helped our cause, it didn't matter."

"And he did help, didn't he. It was through Helmut that the Soviet bloc funneled money to your group."

She didn't answer with words, but she didn't have to. She gave it away with her eyes and her fingers on the coffee cup.

"Helmut was your control advisor. Who was his? Sir Marcus Loring?"

She laughed. "That fat old fool? Everyone knew he was an ass."

"Then why did you follow him?"

"I didn't. None of us did. He was very rich and he had contacts all over the world. He made a good figurehead for the party."

"Did you ever meet Helmut's London control?"

"No."

Carter took a drag on his cigarette to hide his elation. "But you must have been with him, at least in the area, when he met her?"

"Yes, but she never spoke. I only heard the man's voice, and then nothing was discussed. I never saw either one of their faces."

"But it was the same man that recruited you?"

"Yes."

"And you never saw his face, then?"

"No."

"But you're sure he's working in the best interests of your cause," Carter said, keeping his face a mask.

"Yes."

"Did you know that if the two people would have reached here, Helmut had orders to kill them?"

"Impossible! He told me himself that they were not to be harmed in any way."

"Are you sure he didn't just tell you that in order to calm any fears you might have?"

More silence, but Carter knew he had hit a nerve. He decided on one last zinger.

"One more thing . . ."

"What?"

"You had already passed out from the gas, but do you realize that when we crashed the lodge, Helmut was not shooting that shotgun at *us?*"

"What do you mean?"

"I mean, it was no accident that Wolfgang was wounded. If we had not shot Helmut, he would have killed you all."

The color drained from her face and the cup suddenly started rattling in the saucer. Carter mashed out his cigarette and leaned forward, putting his elbows on the table.

"Want to tell me the rest of it now, Roberta?"

She started slowly, her voice squeaky and hesitant, but it wasn't long before the words poured from her mouth.

By the time Carter joined the others, they were all smiling.

"Did you hear it all?"

"Every word," Keller replied.

"How soon can you get us back to the airfield?"

"Less than an hour," Reinbold said. "I'll call ahead to have your plane ready."

Miriam turned to Carter as they walked to the car. "How did you know the London contact was a woman?"

"I didn't, and it wasn't . . . at least, not completely. It was a couple. I just figured that Roberta would jump one way or the other if I tagged the contact as a woman. It was just a lucky pop."

"It's hard to imagine."

"Why?"

Miriam shook her head. "It just is, that's all. Abby Sinclair is not that smart. And she might be a strong liberal, but she's not strong enough to chance her neck in a noose."

"We'll see what Henderson has gotten out of them as soon as we get back to London."

Carla stood and stretched her aching muscles. Nearby, Norman Dufont did the same.

"Is that it?" he asked.

"That's more than it." She smiled broadly. "Moscow will make generals of the both of us."

"Major Gorokhov!"

The door opened at once, and the blond KGB major stepped stiffly into the room. "*Da*, comrade?"

"We have finished. A complete success. Put both of them in the van."

"*Da*, comrade."

For the next two hours, the old Georgian mansion was a flurry of activity. The tapes were transferred to much more compact wire recordings, and the originals were burned. Sir John Hillary and Mildred Hastings were placed in the back of a white van.

Eventually they were all standing between the green Jaguar and the van in the arc of the drive.

Dufont issued orders.

"Major, you know where to meet us."

"Of course."

"Volcek, you and your men go over the house. I want it left just as it was, just as you found it when you arrived."

"*Da,* comrade."

"You have your passports and tickets?"

"*Da,* comrade. There is a flight from Edinburgh early in the morning for Paris. We will change papers at Orly and board Aeroflot for Moscow then."

"Excellent. Congratulate yourselves, gentlemen. You have just pulled off one of the major espionage coups of all time. You will be rewarded accordingly."

Norman Dufont held the door for the dark-haired woman, then slid into the driver's seat.

"You have everything?"

She made a mental check, and then remembered. "The wig!"

Dufont smiled and opened his attaché case. The blond wig, its style only slightly in disarray, was inside.

"Probably the first minor thing I have ever seen you slip up on."

She smiled. "Blame it on weariness."

"You're entitled. Shall we go?"

"Let's . . . and get the rest of it over with as quickly as possible."

TWELVE

Because of the Copeland's size and its lack of ultrasophisticated radar, fog and heavy storms over the Channel delayed them. It was nearly three o'clock in the afternoon before Carter and Miriam set down at Gatwick and taxied to the private sector. There, they dashed through the downpour toward a helicopter, only to be told that it would be impossible to take off in less than an hour; more than likely, it would be two.

"Dammit! Get us a car, fast!" Carter growled.

A Special Branch man was found and a car was secured.

It was nearly five o'clock by the time they arrived in London and walked into the operations center at Cavendish Square.

Giles Henderson looked like a dead man. Seeing him brought home to Carter his own lack of sleep.

What Henderson had to report didn't serve to perk up either himself or Miriam Lockwood.

"We've interrogated everyone in our files that had even the slightest brush with the People's Party."

"And they know nothing," Carter said.

"That's right. Of course, there is an element of the party

we don't know, sort of an undercover arm. Only Sir Marcus Loring had a list of those names.''

"What about his widow . . . what's her name?"

"Lady Phyllis Loring. We've interrogated her as well. It seems she wasn't exactly in tune with her husband politically. In fact, we got it from friends and neighbors that she and Sir Marcus were on the verge of a crack-up."

"And so far there have been no ransom demands?" Miriam asked.

"None, and none of the usual 'we take responsibility' phone calls from any other terrorist groups."

Carter rubbed his eyes and tried to make his weary mind work. "If their demands are that missiles be pulled out of England and Europe, I would think they would have said so by now."

"I would think so," Giles Henderson agreed. "By the way, that L-type launch belonging to Cleaves was named and registered as *The Raven*. Cleaves's brother says he was thick with a man called Izzy for the past few weeks. He gave us a good description. We've already flashed it around."

"What have you done on the info from the German girl, Roberta Kirsch?"

Henderson winced at the question. "We've already interrogated Abby Sinclair and Jason Eldridge until we're blue in the face and they're burning mad. To tell you the truth, they came out clean as a whistle."

"What about Abby's comment at the party?" Miriam said.

"You mean, to the effect that Mildred Hastings was about to get hers?"

"Yes."

Henderson's face flushed slightly. "Well, it seems that she was alluding to a little fling Mrs. Hastings was having."

"What kind of a fling?" Carter asked.

"Isn't there just one kind?"

"An affair?"

Henderson nodded. "It's with a younger man, and somehow Abby Sinclair found out about it. She planned to expose it to the press."

"Who's the man?"

"Fellow by the name of Norman Dufont. Cambridge, old family, money, all the right connections. As it turns out, Mrs. Hastings wasn't the least worried about any scandal. It was Dufont who wanted to keep the affair quiet."

"You've talked to him?"

"No, he's on holiday . . . a hunting trip somewhere in Scotland. We got the story from Mrs. Hastings's housekeeper."

Carter yawned. "But you've got the Sinclair woman and Jason Eldridge under surveillance?"

"Twenty-four-hour watchers, but I really don't think it will do much good."

"It's all we have right now," Carter replied. "Roberta Kirsch heard the London contact call his lady friend Abby. To me that's pretty damning, and it points to Jason Eldridge as our man."

"You're out on your feet," Henderson said, "both of you. Why don't you cave in? I'll ring you if anything breaks."

"A brilliant idea," Miriam groaned, and Carter didn't argue.

Henderson stopped them at the door of the office. "Uh, where . . . uh . . ."

"Yes?"

"Where should I ring you?"

Carter and Miriam glanced at each other. They didn't need words. Their weariness was in their eyes.

"I'll be at the Soho apartment," Carter said. "You've got the number."

"Righto."

Miriam dropped him within a block and Carter stumbled to the AXE safe house.

He stripped, showered, shaved, and fell into bed. Just

before sleep claimed him, he made a mental note to do a little snooping and interrogating himself later that evening.

Roberta Kirsch had been scared. She had been sure of that name. Abby Sinclair had to fit somewhere.

It was just past midnight when Norman Dufont pulled the Jaguar off the highway into the Harrow Road rest stop. It was completely empty other than the white van.

He killed the lights and then sat for a full two minutes. Satisfied that there were no hitchhiking travelers bunking down for the night in the nearby trees, he got out.

The movement was a signal to Gorokhov, who quickly joined him in the rear of the van.

Wordlessly they transferred the two sleeping figures to the rear seat of the Jaguar. They were placed on the seat and then toppled over so one would have to be standing right beside the car to see them.

The two men moved back to the van and shook hands.

"Congratulations, Colonel Dufont. It has been a pleasure serving you."

"You have done an excellent job, Gorokhov. Leave the keys to the van under the mat when you reach Heathrow. It will be picked up."

"I shall see you in Paris in a week's time."

Gorokhov climbed into the van and sped away. Dufont went to the trunk of the Jag and opened the lid. Quickly he shifted the license plates and slammed the lid again.

By the time he slid back under the wheel, the woman had donned the blond wig and combed it out.

"Are they still out?"

"Sleeping like babes."

Dufont started the car, and twenty minutes later he was in The Dells, pulling into Dellmar Close.

Martha White sat in front of the television with her husband, Baldwin, watching the late news.

It was boring, and Mr. White was already nodding.

The moment Martha heard the car, she lurched to her feet and scampered to the front window. So abrupt was her movement that it jolted the drowsy Mr. White to wakefulness.

Carefully, the woman made a crack in the drapes so she could see.

"Well, the love nest will be put to good use again tonight!"

Mr. White groaned. His wife was an inveterate snoop and gossip.

"That Sinclair woman's a real hussy, she is!"

She watched the Jaguar go into the garage and the door slowly close. But not before she saw the blond head reflected in the gleam of the lights.

Martha White knew that Number 12 was being rented by the widow of an ex-M.P. from Devon, Abby Sinclair, because Hattie Ellis had told her so. Hattie Ellis should know. She was as big a snoop as Martha White, and she was the wife of Jonathan Ellis, the realtor who handled the management of The Dells.

"Let's go to bed, Martha," Mr. White declared with a grunt, rising from his chair.

"I don't know why the woman can't have her affairs in London like the rest of them loose women. Bringin' her lovers up here like that . . . it's a scandal to the neighborhood, it is!"

"Lovers? You mean this is a new one?"

"Nah, same one. Drivin' that same green Jaguar car, he is. I knows it by the license plate."

"Martha, let's go to bed."

Together they muscled Mildred Hastings and Sir John Hillary from the car and up the stairs into the two bedrooms. Once they were deposited on the beds, they checked the house just to make sure that not even a stray hair had been left lying around.

There was little need. Each time they had been in the

house, they had worn gloves and moved in carefully defined areas.

They didn't bother to do the dishes or tidy up the mess they had purposely made. It must look, to Special Branch, as though several people had spent at least three days in the house.

"Do you think they'll buy it?" she asked.

"They will, for a few days at least, and that's all we'll need."

Back in the garage, Dufont used the automatic opener on the door and slid the Jag back into the street.

Martha White's radarlike ears caught the sound of the garage door sliding up the instant it started. She lay in bed for several seconds, and then she could stand it no longer.

Throwing her legs over the side of the bed, she padded quickly to the window.

She was just in time to see the garage door close and the taillights of the Jaguar turning out of Dellmar Close.

"Well now, that'un was a quickie, weren't it?"

"What are you ravin' about now, woman?"

"The Sinclair whore. She and her lover man are leavin' already, they are!"

"Dammit to hell, woman, will you come back to bed?"

"Aye, to bed I will. But I tell you, I'm talkin' to Hattie in the mornin'."

"What on earth for?"

"To find out when her lease is up, that's what for. All this illicit fornicatin' in the neighborhood has got to stop!"

Mr. White rolled onto his side, away from his wife.

He guessed that the fornicating that went on at Number 12 was the only exercise of that kind going on in the whole neighborhood.

He knew it was a lot more than was going on in his own house.

Mr. White had seen pictures of Abby Sinclair in the newspaper. He wished he was ten years or so younger. He'd love to meet his neighbor in Number 12.

Just before pulling onto the M1 motorway, Dufont again changed the license plates.

"It will be a pity not to drive this gem anymore," he said, joining the speeding traffic toward London.

"Well, I won't be sorry to get rid of this," she said, pulling the wig off and shaking out her raven hair. "I think I'll burn it in celebration."

They chuckled to themselves all the way to Hyde Park. Dufont stopped the car in the shadows between two street-lights and leaned in front of her to open the door.

"I'll see you in Paris, luv," he said, lightly brushing her cheeks with his lips.

"Paris it is," she replied, and stepped from the car.

He watched her walk under the arch and turn into the parking lot adjacent to St. George's Hospital. Two minutes later a gray BMW darted from the gate. She waved as she passed him, and Dufont waved back.

Before heading on up Oxford Street, he ground his fingers into his eyes. They felt as if they were full of sand. He was dead tired and would have liked to spend the next twelve hours in a soft bed, starting right now.

But the night's work was far from over.

At last he pulled the gear lever into drive, and the Jag headed smoothly and silently up Oxford Street. At South-ampton Row, he turned left into the Bloomsbury district. Just past Russell Square, he rolled down to the underground gate of Chubb's Garage.

Just before the attendant opened the door, he slipped the garage door opener from Number 12 Dellmar Close into his jacket pocket.

"Mornin', sir."

"Good morning. Have them give it a good wash, will you, and vacuum the seats?"

"I'll do that, sir."

Dufont pressed a fiver into his hand and walked back up to the street. He walked around the square and entered the VIP lot in the rear of the British Museum. His four-year-old Volvo was one of four cars in the lot. The museum VIP sticker in the window was a special favor from Mildred.

She had seen that he had gotten it when he complained that it took him longer to park than to do the research he needed for the book he was writing.

He chuckled as he steered the Volvo from the lot. He had been working on the book for five years, and no one ever expected him to publish it. The actual writing took too much time away from his life as a London bon vivant.

His first stop was the *Times* building, where he dropped a dark manila envelope marked "Urgent: Night Editor" through the deposit slit for night mail deliveries.

From there he drove across London to Portland Place and Broadcasting House. BBC-1 and BBC-2 each had slits for night mail delivery. He dropped identical envelopes through them both.

From Broadcasting House, it was a ten-minute drive to his own apartment in Upper Brook Street across from Grosvenor Square. Just before pulling into his subterranean garage, he saluted the statue of Franklin Delano Roosevelt in the square and the lighted windows of the American embassy across the square.

He had always thought it a bit ironic that he lived in this location. But, of course, there was more than irony in the choice.

Jason Eldridge lived in the same apartment building.

The night guard waved and opened his tiny window. "Welcome home, Mr. Dufont. How did you do?"

"Didn't hit a thing, George. Think I'm getting old."

He parked his car and headed for the elevator. When he was out of the old man's sight, he darted between cars to a dark green Jaguar sedan.

With the skill that a master car thief would appreciate, Dufont had the car door open in eleven seconds. He replaced the garage door opener on the visor, relocked the car, and took the elevator to his apartment.

Once inside, he thankfully pulled the driving gloves from his sweaty hands. It was one of only three times the gloves had been off in the last forty-eight hours.

He poured a scotch, neat, and drank it down. With a second drink, he moved across the room to the telephone.

He had several numbers to call, but he didn't have to consult a book. He knew them all very well by heart.

The first call was picked up on the first ring, and the hoarse, aging voice of the man who answered was alert and wide awake.

"Yes?"

"I have the materials."

"I will be in the shop just before eight."

"There are fourteen spools. Can you still finish in time?"

"I will have to, won't I?" the man replied with a chuckle, and hung up.

It took ten full rings before the second call was answered by a very sleepy female voice.

"Double-ought-nine-two."

"Hello, Gertrude, Norman Dufont here. Sorry to wake you at this hour, but I promised Mildred I would ring her up the moment I got back to London."

"Oh, uh . . . Mr. Dufont, yes . . ."

"Don't tell me you've forgotten me in three days, old girl! Put Mildred on, will you?"

"Well, uh . . . Mr. Dufont . . ."

"Is anything wrong, Gertrude?"

"No, no, sir, nothing at all, sir. But Mrs. Hastings isn't here.."

"Isn't there?"

"No, sir. She had to go down to the country. Some trouble there with the tenants."

"Oh, bother! They can be a pain, can't they?"

"Yes, sir, yes, sir, they certainly can, sir."

"Well, tell her I called and that I'll ring her up when she returns."

"I'll do that, sir. Good night."

"Good night, Gertrude."

Norman Dufont was almost laughing out loud as he dialed his third and final call.

"Hello?"

"You got in all right."

"Yes, I was just stepping into a bath. Everything done?"

"To perfection."

"Marvelous," she replied. "Wish me well for tomorrow."

"Brompton Cemetery, isn't it?"

"Yes."

"I know you'll mourn well, darling. Good night."

"Good night."

Giles Henderson came bolt upright from the cot on the first ring, his hand groping for the phone on the nearby desk.

"Henderson here."

"Boyle, sir."

"Boyle, Boyle . . . ah, yes, go ahead."

Ian Boyle was the special tech man in the basement of Mildred Hastings's building. He was the night listener on the woman's phone tap.

"Norman Dufont is back in London, sir. He just talked to the housekeeper. Wanted to speak to Mrs. Hastings."

"Then he doesn't know."

"Doesn't sound like it, sir."

"What did the housekeeper tell him?"

"Just your instructions, sir . . . the missus is in the country—tenant problems."

"Good. Thank you, Boyle."

"Yes, sir."

Henderson had scarcely replaced the receiver when it jangled again.

"Yes?"

"Sir, I have the *Times* for you on line three."

"The London *Times?*"

"Yes, sir."

Henderson felt sweat pop out on his forehead and the back of his neck. "Put them through."

"Yes, sir. You're on to Special Branch . . . Mr. Henderson, sir."

"Henderson, this is Wallace Wade, chief editor, *Times* night desk."

"Yes, Mr. Wade. What can I do for you?"

"I think it's more a case of what I can do for you . . ."

Henderson didn't take a single breath throughout the rest of the man's speech. Wade read the declaration from the People's Party for Peace, and then read it again at Henderson's insistence.

"Stand on it, Wade," Henderson gasped at last. "I don't want another soul to see it."

"It's news, Henderson."

"It also falls under the Official Secrets Act."

"Christ, what doesn't these days?"

"Just stand on it! I'll have a man there in five minutes to pick it up!"

The connection was barely broken before the operator was back on the line.

"I have the BBC on line one, sir . . ."

THIRTEEN

The shop was one of many just like it on Lower Thames Street, two blocks from London Bridge. Norman Dufont was at the door at eight o'clock sharp, eyeing the hand-lettered sign through the foggy glass: KLAUSSERMAN IMPORTED JEWELRY, Hours 9-7, Mon.-Sat.''

Dufont rang the bell, and from a small room in the rear of the shop a little man shuffled through a frayed curtain. He was in his middle fifties, short and plump, bald except for a crescent of hair above each ear and a few strands slicked obliquely over the top of his head. His clean-shaven face was round, with small eyes behind thick glasses, and he moved with a practiced air of cheerful mediocrity.

"Yes?"

"Herr Klausserman?"

"Yes."

"I am your Red Star connection," Dufont whispered.

"Step in, please." Dufont did, and the door was quickly closed and locked behind him. "My assistant doesn't come in until nine, but we'll use the back room just in case. This way."

The shop was small, clean, and slightly shabby, touched for too many years by the grime of open fires during London winters. It was the kind of shop where low-fare European and American tourists shopped for high-quality craftsmanship at rock-bottom prices.

The back room was severe, with a single chair and a jeweler's workbench and high stool under a low hanging lamp. On the table, Klausserman's tools were carefully laid out.

"You have the materials?"

"I do."

Dufont opened his briefcase and set two black rectangular boxes on the worktable. The old man opened both of them and extracted one of the reels.

He ran a couple of feet of the magnetic wire recording off the spool and inspected it minutely.

"How many spools?"

"Fourteen, .05 grain."

Klausserman nodded. "I can see that. They will have to be treated before I can put the gold plating around them. I have already fashioned the clasp, so that will be no problem.

"Do you have a sketch of the necklace?"

The old man moved to a small floor safe, spun its dial, and reached inside. He returned to the table with a manila folder. Inside was a sheet of onion skin.

"The number of strands I have sketched will be sufficient to accommodate that much wire if I alter the dimensions slightly, here."

"And the weight?"

"Will hardly change."

"Excellent," Dufont said. "Now, the time. You know my limitations."

Klausserman nodded and did some calculations on a white pad. When he seemed satisfied, he turned back to Dufont.

"This is Monday. Your flight leaves from Gatwick to Paris at three Wednesday afternoon. Correct?"

"Yes."

"It will take some doing, but I can have it ready by noon on Wednesday."

Dufont bit his lip. "A daylight delivery may involve you later, when the necklace disappears in France."

"That is true, but we have no choice. Shall we say a newspaper swap in St. James's Park, on the Victoria Memorial side?"

"Very well. Noon Wednesday," Dufont replied, closing his briefcase.

Klausserman smiled. "It will be an exquisite piece. I am sure the lady will be overjoyed."

Dufont laughed aloud. "I am sure she will . . . for as long as she has it."

Major Gorokhov checked out of the White Horse Hotel in Staines at eight-thirty. He wore jeans, a lightweight shirt, and a brown leather jacket, and carried a small overnight case. He looked and sounded in his speech in perfect accordance with the occupation on his passport: miner.

It was a fifteen-minute cab ride to Heathrow, where he approached the British Airways counter and presented his passport.

"I got a seat on the ten-thirty to Orly, mate," he said, a wide smile on his boyish face. "Gonna have a bit of a lark in Pigalle tonight, I am!"

"Yes, sir, Mr. Packman. Smoking or nonsmoking?"

"Nonsmokin'. I give 'em up."

"Only the one bag, sir?"

"Righto, I'll carry it on."

"There you are, sir. Seat Twenty-three A. The flight starts boarding at ten o'clock. You can clear customs right now if you like."

"Righto."

He moved through the crowds to the international barriers, and again handed over his passport.

The uniformed customs agent eyed the passport, then checked its photograph with the blond-haired man standing before him.

"Holiday or business in France, Mr. Packman?"

"Bit of a holiday."

Gorokhov's mind was Russian, trained in Soviet ways. Since he constantly mistrusted everyone and everything around him, it was easy for him to spot mistrust or caution in the eyes of another.

He saw both these qualities in the eyes of the customs man as he checked picture against face a second and then a third time.

Finally the ticket, boarding pass, and stamped passport were returned.

"Have a nice holiday, Mr. Packman."

"Thank you."

Gorokhov moved into the boarding area with all his faculties on alert. At first he sensed them. Then he could practically smell them closing in.

One—short, heavyset, and powerful—set his paper down and moved toward him. Another came out of a "Private Sector" door. He barely glanced at Gorokhov, but moved in an arc toward him.

Across the barrier, he saw two more moving slowly across the lobby toward the boarding area.

There was no doubt about it. He had been made, maybe blown.

"Excuse me, mate, but do you have a light?" The one on his left.

Gorokhov barely turned his head that way, when the bag was deftly lifted from his right hand and that wrist was locked in a viselike grip.

A millisecond later, the one on his left did the same to his left wrist.

" 'Ere now . . ." Gorokhov muttered, determined to maintain the charade for as long as possible.

"We'd like to talk to you, Mr. Packman." A badge was flashed before his eyes. "Special Branch, Scotland Yard."

"If you'll just come this way, Mr. Packman, we'll try not to inconvenience you any more than a few moments."

" 'Ere, I ain't done nothin' . . ."

But he was being moved skillfully and forcefully toward the barrier. The two dark-suited men already there were clearing the way for them.

Little bells went off in Gorokhov's mind. "Who are them two blokes?"

One of them answered for both. "I'm Pearson, and this is Agent Harris, MI5. We would just like to ask you a few questions, Mr. Packman."

Bullshit, Gorokhov thought.

He was a trained agent and, as such, knew British law and procedure. MI5 was counterintelligence. By law, they did not exist as a police agency. They could not make an arrest. If they considered an arrest necessary, officers of Scotland Yard or its Special Branch had to be called in to make that arrest.

With both agencies on the scene, there was little doubt in Gorokhov's mind.

He was definitely under arrest.

He remembered clearly the words of General Kiertov, his Moscow control: *Operation Red Star is of vast importance. It has been in the planning stages for over two years. Each link could be the one to break the entire operation. No link must be broken, Major, at any time.*

Gorokhov knew full well the general's meaning.

He was fast, too fast, for all four of them, even as highly trained as they were. He jammed his heel down on the instep of the one on his right. In the same movement, he round-housed the one on his left and broke free from the clutching hands of the two men from MI5.

People parted like the sea in front of a boat's prow as he ran headlong through the corridor. Wildly, his eyes darted from one side to the other.

He knew escape was hopeless. If he managed to make the parking lot, the airport police would get him in minutes.

He only needed a few seconds of privacy.

Over his shoulder he could see three of the four bearing down on him. Another two minutes and they would have him.

And then he saw the door marked "Gentlemen" in four languages. He darted through, and paused. A long line of urinals on his left, washbasins and mirrors on his right. Six booths in the rear.

He bolted.

The first two booths were occupied. He slammed into the third and locked the door. It only took him two seconds to unhinge the false tooth. He didn't even have to take it out of his mouth. All he did was flip it until the capsule fell out.

He shifted it to the other side of his mouth and bit down, hard.

Mildred Hastings felt feeling first in her fingers and toes. As the rest of her body slowly came to life, she managed to blink one eye open.

Gray light filtered across her face through partially open paisley drapes. Mildred's mind instantly registered the god-awful color. It didn't agree with the wallpaper at all.

And then she realized.

Where in God's name am I?

She tried to rise, but her muscles ached. She was breathing hard and the air that entered her lungs was stale. Her hands moved, exploring.

Dear God, she was fully clothed, and in a bed.

Using all her willpower, she began moving, one piece at a time. To her relief, her limbs answered at last the hazy commands of her brain. Her arms and legs weren't broken, they just felt that way, and her spine was intact.

She moistened her lips with a thick, dry tongue, and managed a sitting position. Immediately, nausea overwhelmed her.

Keep at it, old girl, keep at it, she told herself. *This, too, shall pass.*

Her stomach muscles knotted painfully when she tried to sit up. But she managed it, and another move that let her feet find the floor. Then she was no longer afraid of dying.

Now she was afraid she might not die, and that thought sent her stumbling to the bath. Once there, she embraced the commode like a lover and thought what a ridiculous picture she must make. At last there was only the bitter taste of bile in her mouth, but her body continued to shake from the spasms.

Gripping the sink, Mildred pulled herself to her feet, turned on the cold water, and stuck her head under the faucet. With her wet head dripping cold water, she examined herself in the mirror.

Good God, old girl, you look like a Tottenham whore . . . or what's left of one. Your hair is a mess, you . . .

Hair!

And then she remembered. She swiveled her head from side to side and saw the scratches behind her ears.

In panic, she lurched from the bath. The more she moved, the clearer her head became.

Don't panic, she told herself, but she almost did when she heard a groan through the open door to her left.

And then another groan. A man's groan.

She whirled around and spotted a set of fireplace tools.

Clutching a poker in both hands, she moved stealthily into the hall toward the sounds.

It was another bedroom, even more appallingly decorated than the one she had just awakened in. An older man sat on the side of the bed, his thick head of graying hair cradled in his hands.

"Make one move and I'll brain you!" Mildred yelped.

"What's that . . . Mildred . . . ?"

"Dear God . . . Sir John!"

There was a tapping on the door, and Carter spiraled to the surface of consciousness. Outside the window, he saw gray light.

Good God, he thought, *I've slept the night away.*

He lay there, trying to absorb the facts that had troubled his sleep and bring himself to an alert state.

The tapping sounded again.

Carter rolled, aching, from the bed and lurched to the door.

"Who is it?"

"Your fairy godmother."

He jerked the door open and Miriam walked past him. She paused at the dresser and started doing things with paper cups.

She was wearing a green jersey dress that clung tenaciously to every hill and hollow of her glorious body. Her magnificent breasts pushed themselves against the soft material as if it were a personal insult to them. Her movement was pure undulation, a delicious study in female locomotion.

And then she was there, passing him a cup and running a finger lightly, caressingly, along the line of his jaw.

"What are you smiling at?"

"You, what a marvelous thing to wake up to. Is it morning or afternoon?"

"Just noon."

He sipped the coffee. "I slept . . . hard."

"I know. I called you twice from Cavendish and there was no answer. Henderson and I decided to handle everything and let you sleep."

"Thanks. What's new?"

She explained the written demands from the People's Party that had been delivered earlier to the *Times*, BBC-1, and BBC-2.

"According to them, there are no demands. Sir John Hillary and Mildred Hastings were kidnapped and detained only as a symbolic act, a statement of the People's Party's opposition to U.S. missiles in Europe.''

''And . . .?''

''And they have not been harmed, and they will be released soon.''

Carter lit a cigarette and let the smoke burn his lungs enough to clear his brain. ''But no clue as to where to find them?''

''None.''

''And no demand for ransom . . . like the withdrawal of the missiles?''

''No, actually it was a pretty calm statement.''

The phone jangled and he grabbed it. ''Carter here.''

''Nick, this is Henderson. We got Izzy at the airport. He was headed for Orly on a U.K. passport in the name of I.L. Packman.''

''Terrific. I'll shower and get right over. Have you started interrogation yet?''

''No. And you can take your time with your shower. He's dead.''

''Dead?''

''Locked himself in a men's room stall and bit down on a cyanide capsule. By the time the MI5 boys got over the stall door, he was already dead.''

''Shit.''

''My sentiments exactly. We've already got a make on him through an Identakit photo. It matches a shot taken in East Germany about four years ago. In reality, 'Izzy' is Major Illya Vassilovitch Gorokhov. As near as we can guess, he's attached to the First Directorate.''

''KGB . . .''

''Right, and a big gun, only used sparingly. He was expertly trained, with an English specialty.''

''Hmm, interesting,'' Carter growled, his mind racing. ''Anything else?''

''Nothing. If Miriam's there, she's told you all the rest.''

"Yeah. We'll check in later."

"Righto."

Carter hung up and briefed her quickly.

"I'll grab a shower."

"All right. It's odd, though . . ." she said, her pretty brow furrowed in thought.

"What?"

"This Gorokhov. High-priority agent and all that. They don't waste those boys. And to kill himself? I mean, they know as well as we do that he could have been jailed as a spy, but he probably would have been traded for someone eventually. It's damned odd he would opt to off himself."

"Yeah," Carter agreed, "I was thinking the same thing myself. I'm going to clear my head with a shower."

He ran it cold, then hot, then cold again before he even started to soap his body.

It *was* odd, he thought, that Gorokhov would choose to kill himself rather than take his chances and be traded back to Moscow.

Odd, that is, unless he wanted to avoid an interrogation at all cost.

"There are tots in the streets and women jawing in their front yards," Sir John Hillary said, peering through a crack in the front drapes.

"At least we're still in England," Mildred replied.

"Yes, and the house is empty."

"Why don't we just walk out?"

"No, I don't think we ought to do that. Here now . . ." Sir John walked to the phone and picked it up. "I'll be damned."

"What?"

"The bloody thing's working!" Quickly he dialed 911.

"Harrow Emergency, Sergeant Harcourt here."

"Sergeant, this is Major General Sir John Hillary."

"Sure it is, guv, an' I'll be chief constable by week's

end."

"I *am* General Hillary, dammit, and I'm with Mrs. Mildred Hastings, M.P. from Devon. We don't know where we are."

"Jesus Christ. Stay on the phone, sir, I'll have the call traced!"

Carter heard the ring as he stepped from the shower. Miriam was just hanging up when he entered the room. The expression on her face told him the news was big.

"What is it?"

"Sir John and Mrs. Hastings have just surfaced . . ."

"Where?"

"A house in Harrow. Henderson is sending a car."

"Are they all right?"

"Yes," she nodded numbly. "It seems they just woke up and called the local constable."

The overcast was still heavy, but the drizzle had stopped by the time the final words had been uttered over the remains of Sir Marcus Loring.

Considering his wealth and status, there were very few people at the grave site. Besides the widow and the man of the cloth, there were a few reporters from the dailies, some servants, and one distinguished-looking couple. The woman was a tall, fortyish, aristocratic blonde, and the man beside her smacked equally of class in an expensive coat and bowler.

The two teen-agers were gasping for breath as they entered the cemetery gates. They had run all the way from the West Brompton station.

"Thank God, Davey, the funeral party is still there! See 'em by the grave?"

"Aye, I see 'em."

"Well, let's go!"

"Go where? We can see 'em good enough from here."

"Damn you, Davey, you're the one who said we couldn't be sure from just a black-and-white news photo . . ."

"Well, we couldn't."

"Well, we're here to see fer sure now, in the flesh. C'mon!"

Reluctantly, the boy ambled along behind the girl. "Where're you goin'?"

"I'm goin' to get close to the family car so we can see her when she gets in."

"Jeez, Jenny . . ."

"C'mon!" She grasped his hand and pulled him along.

The graveside services had finished, and the widow was being escorted toward the dark Bentley limousine by the aristocratic couple.

"I want to thank you both for coming, Abby . . . Jason."

"Nothing to it, Phyllis dear," the man replied. "Thing to do and all that, you know."

"Call us if you need anything, Phyllis."

"I will, Abby, and thank you."

Just as she was about to step into the car, a hand touched her elbow. She paused and turned full face to look at a young boy and girl.

"Beggin' yer pardon, ma'am," the girl said.

"Yes?"

"Me lad and me, we'd like to offer our sympathies."

"Thank you."

"You are the widow, ain't ya, Lady Phyllis?"

"Yes, I am."

The Bentley pulled away and the rest of the mourners trickled from the cemetery in their own cars. When the last one was out the gate and moving away along Old Brompton Road, the girl turned to the boy.

"Well?"

"Aye, there's little doubt of it. It's her, all right. I'd recognize that face through five veils."

"Then we'll go?"

"Aye, Jenny, we'll go," he replied, "right to Scotland Yard."

FOURTEEN

The reports were strung out across the desk in front of Carter, and he was on the fifth go-round of reading through them.

It didn't make sense, not a damned bit of it.

Special Branch and MI5 people had swarmed into The Dells and covered Number 12 Dellmar Close like the proverbial blanket.

All they found was a perplexed General Sir John Hillary and an angry Mildred Hastings. The couple, after a brief questioning, had been whisked away to the Admiralty Hospital.

Then more questions were asked, depositions were taken, and the roundup had begun.

It all pointed to the People's Party doing just exactly what they had claimed, and Carter, while not believing a single word, couldn't disprove any of it.

Giles Henderson entered the office and wearily lowered his body into a chair.

"Well?" Carter asked, looking up from the reports.

"Abby Sinclair admits to renting the house. She and Eldridge used it for their afternoon trysts."

"Why?"

"Eldridge has an 'arrangement' with his wife . . . Mrs. Eldridge has her own affairs. They just both agreed to do it all discreetly, outside of London."

"Yeah, and only their fingerprints were found all over the house. Damn."

Henderson nodded in agreement. "We've got them dead-on, except for the statement from Mrs. Martha White, the neighbor across the street. She said that Mrs. Sinclair and her lover were there last night for about an hour just past midnight."

"I read her statement in the report," Carter said. "And Abby Sinclair claims she didn't leave her apartment from five in the afternoon until she met Eldridge to go to Loring's funeral today."

"Right. The White woman claims definite identification, but our surveillance boys are just as adamant. They back up Abby Sinclair's story."

Carter slammed his hand on the desk. "It's no good. It's bullshit, a web."

"Yes, it is," Henderson agreed, "but not one we can untangle very quickly."

"Excuse me, sir . . ."

"Yes?" Henderson turned to the young woman at the door.

"Here are the results of the medical tests on Sir John and Mrs. Hastings."

"Thank you."

Carter was deep in his own thoughts on the other side of the desk. Slowly he calmed down and let the analytical side of his trained agent's mind take over.

Obviously, Abby Sinclair and Jason Eldridge had been set up as the masterminds of the kidnapping. It was all just too pat.

Everyone else had been dragged in for interrogation, from

François the hairdresser to Norman Dufont, Mrs. Hastings's young lover.

Nothing.

Had the kidnapped couple been in the house right from the beginning? According to the rather precise statement of Martha White, they must have been. The woman was a catalogue of the green Jaguar's comings and goings. It all fit.

Why the caper in the first place? It accomplished nothing, and ruined the People's Party. Their demands were never even publicized.

There had to be a deeper reason for the kidnappings, especially if the KGB was so deeply involved.

And involved they were. Major Gorokhov was more than adequate proof of that.

"It seems that the general and Mrs. Hastings came through all this in fine fettle."

"How's that?"

"Their medical reports," Henderson said, flipping the pages across the desk.

Absently, Carter's eye fell to the medical diagnosis and blood analysis. He recognized some of the symbols, but not many of the others . . . except one.

Two minutes later he was shouting at an operator in the Admiralty.

"I don't give a damn if he's in conference with the Queen! Put Doctor Lloyd on the line and put him on *now!*"

One minute later an angry voice barked at Carter, "Look here . . ."

"No, *you* look here, Doctor," Carter replied, and he gave him the high-priority of the investigation and Carter's part in it.

"Sorry, what would you like to know?"

"There were massive traces of Demerol residue in the blood, as well as other depressants."

"That's correct."

"What is Correllium C-Nineteen?"

"It's also a depressant, but more like an anesthetic."

"Like, for instance, Sodium Pentothol?"

"Similar, but probably much stronger. We don't know a great deal about it."

"But there were definitely traces of it in their blood?"

"Yes. Couldn't tell how much, though. The Demerol, in those amounts, practically negates it. Wipes the slate clean, so to speak."

Carter was sweating. "You mean they could have been injected with large amounts of Correllium C-Nineteen, but the Demerol destroyed a lot of its residue with its own?"

"Possible, very possible."

"Thank you, Doctor. Thank you very much."

"Got something?" Henderson asked as Carter hung up the phone.

"Maybe. Get me both their files. I mean *everything*, down to their warts."

"What is it?"

"Maybe the real reason for the kidnapping."

"Sergeant Medlin?"

Medlin rolled around in his chair. With the two VIPs safely back at home base, he had been looking forward to an easy shift. "Yeah, what is it?"

"Got a couple of kids down at the desk."

"So, send 'em to juvie."

"No, sir, they're not arrestees, sir."

"Then what the hell are they?"

"Witnesses, sir. They say they'll only talk to the officer in charge, and they want protection."

"Protection? What in God's name for?"

"They say they saw Sir Marcus Loring's body being dumped in the river."

"Jesus, get 'em in here!"

They were young, attractive, and they looked fairly bright.

"What're yer names?"

"Jenny Wright."

"Davey Carpin . . . sir."

"All right, what's this about seeing someone dump Sir Marcus in the Thames?"

Medlin listened.

Then he listened some more.

Then he made them repeat the whole thing.

Then he grabbed the phone.

Carter left Sir John Hillary's room and walked down the hall to see Mildred Hastings. In his hands he carried both their files.

The half hour he had spent with Sir John had been most instructive. The man was a phenomenon. Carter was pretty sure he had the key now, or at least half of it.

He hoped he was right, and that Mildred Hastings could supply the other half.

"Mrs. Hastings?"

"Yes?"

"My name is Nicholas Carter."

"Yes, I know. Sir Richard Witten-Jones was just here. He explained everything. I'll do whatever I can to help."

"Thank you, I appreciate it. I have just talked to Sir John, and learned some interesting things. I have both of your files here, going clear back to your youth up through your public service. I hope you don't mind?"

"Not at all. Anything that will help clear this all up."

"Good. According to your file, for the last year you and three other members of Parliament have been privy to a top-secret foreign operation run through MI6 called Operation Overland."

"Yes. I've been in on Operation Overland practically since its inception. But only in the last year have the results been gratifying enough to keep almost daily tabs on it."

"I understand this," Carter said and nodded. "I had brief

conversations with your fellow M.P.'s, and their overall knowledge of Overland was excellent, but their details were sketchy.''

"Yes. So?''

Carter smiled. ''I assume Sir Richard explained that I have the highest clearance?''

"Yes,'' she said, a quizzical frown coming across her features.

"Then, Mrs. Hastings, I would like to call into play a certain aspect of your biography.''

She smiled knowingly. "You mean my memory?''

"Yes. According to your file, as well as the biography on Sir John Hillary, you both have almost total recall—''

"Completely total recall,'' she corrected him. "I don't know about Sir John, but I have been plagued—or cursed, if you will—by a photographic memory since childhood.''

Carter managed to suppress his elation. ''Then, Mrs. Hastings, I wonder if you would give me the complete details of Operation Overland.''

Carter had a complete dossier from Sir Richard Witten-Jones on Operation Overland on his lap. For the next forty minutes, he listened to the woman speak, and followed that dossier practically word for word.

"Thank you, Mrs. Hastings. I think you've given me the last piece in the puzzle.''

"Then you know what's been going on? . . . what happened to us?''

"Yes, ma'am. I know *what* . . . now all I have to find out is *who*.''

She chuckled. "Please do it by Wednesday, won't you? I've been planning a fortnight's holiday in France for weeks. And, damn this mess, I'll take it one way or the other.''

"I'll try, Mrs. Hastings . . . I'll do everything I can.''

In the hall, Carter was stopped at the nurses' station.

"Are you Mr. Carter . . . Mr. Nicholas Carter?''

"Yes, I am.''

"A Mr. Henderson has been desperately trying to reach you, sir. You can use that phone there, line two."

Carter poked the appropriate button. "Carter here."

"Giles Henderson, Nick. We've got a bombshell. Medlin just called me from Scotland Yard. He's got a couple of kids down there who claim they were eyewitnesses to the disposal of Sir Marcus Loring's body."

"Can they identify?"

"You bet your ass they can, and have. Try the widow, Lady Phyllis Loring."

"Jesus. Get someone . . . no, *several* someones, on her right away. And check around. I want to know where she was those days that Hastings and Hillary were missing. I mean *every minute*."

"Will do."

Carter slammed the phone down and headed for the elevator. He was pretty sure he now had the *who*.

"Is the Copeland ready?" Carter asked.

"Yes, we had it flown up from Gatwick earlier. Captain Garfield hasn't even left the plane. When they go, we go."

Carter nodded and peered through the field glasses.

"Here they come."

Henderson's eyes went to his own binoculars.

Mildred Hastings and Norman Dufont stepped off the minibus and climbed, arm in arm, up the ladder into the British Airways plane.

Carter checked his watch. It was 2:50.

"Jesus, it's hard to imagine," Henderson hissed.

"What?"

"Dufont, if it is him. I mean, he's old English family, right as rain."

"So was Kim Philby," Carter said drily.

The wheels had really started moving after he had talked to the two teen-agers. A full rundown had turned up nothing on Lady Phyllis Loring, but some discreet inquiries were made.

She was absent for two days of the time Hastings and Hillary were being held. She had gone off ''to be alone,'' according to her solicitor.

Dufont, because another discreet inquiry was made, was also checked out. He, too, was absent during the same time: a hunting trip in Scotland.

The last nail in the two coffins came when Sir Richard Witten-Jones found out that Dufont had first-class seats on the same Paris flight as Mildred Hastings. The final nut screwed tight when a tourist-class reservation was also made on that flight by Lady Phyllis Loring.

''There's the bereaved widow.''

''I see her.''

A second minibus had pulled up to the ramp. Tall, svelte, and beautiful, Lady Phyllis Loring walked up to the door and entered the plane.

''God, I hope Mrs. Hastings has nothing to do with this,'' Henderson said.

''I doubt if she does. I just think she is unknowingly helping get the information out of the country.''

''I still think we should have warned her.''

''No,'' Carter growled. ''She's not that good an actress. No one is. If she let on to Dufont, he would have buried it all and found another way.''

The two of them watched the plane intently. At last the door closed and the chocks were removed from the wheels. Minutes later, the engines roared and the tail started swinging around.

''There they go.''

''And so do we. C'mon!''

French SDECE agents met them with four teams, transportation, and communications at Orly. Carter knew already that reservations had been made for Mildred Hastings and Norman Dufont at the George V. The French secret police were doing a phone-down on every other major hotel in Paris to locate where Lady Phyllis Loring would be staying.

The two taxis diverged just inside the city. Carter and two of the teams followed Mildred Hastings and Dufont. Henderson, with the other two French teams, stuck with Lady Phyllis.

As he expected, they taxied directly to the George V.

"Do we have people on the inside?" Carter asked.

"*Oui, monsieur*. The staff is infiltrated down to the kitchen help."

"Good. We wait and watch."

It was quicker than Carter expected. Less than an hour later, Dufont left the George V and hailed a taxi.

"Stay with him," Carter said, grabbing a mini-radio from one of the French agents. "I'm going in!"

Ten minutes later he was rapping on Mildred Hastings's suite.

She opened the door herself. "Mr. Carter . . . what on earth?"

As gently as possible, Carter shut the door behind him and guided her by the elbow back into the suite.

"Sit down, Mrs. Hastings. I've something to tell you that's going to both anger and disappoint you. But it has to be said. Tell me, how long have you known Norman Dufont?"

"Quite some time," she replied, and then laughed. "Oh, come now. If you think my little-May-December romance has some sort of national repercussions, that's absurd!"

"I'm afraid not, Mrs. Hastings," Carter replied quietly.

He told her, in deliberate detail, everything he knew and everything he guessed. By the time he had finished, tears were creeping from the corners of her eyes and her head had shrunk between her shoulders.

"I've been a silly old woman," she said at last.

"Quite the opposite," Carter chuckled. "I think you're an attractive and obviously very vital woman. And if Dufont is our man, a lot of people—English people—were fooled for a lot of years by Kim Philby as well."

His words had managed to bring just the tiniest suggestion

of a smile to the corners of her mouth as she looked up. "What can I do?"

"You can tell me anything and everything Norman Dufont has said to you—or done with you—since his first visit with you in the Admiralty Hospital after you were released."

"Everything?" she asked.

"Everything," he countered.

She did, and it amounted to exactly nothing, zip . . . one great big, very large zero.

Carter lit a cigarette and leaned back into the plush sofa with a sigh.

"Oh, wait," she said, "there was one more thing. In the cab on the way to Heathrow, Norman gave me a very lovely present. It was for the first anniversary of our little . . . liaison."

"What was that?" he asked.

"A beautiful necklace of gold chains."

"Could I see that necklace, Mrs. Hastings?"

"Of course," she replied, and walked into the bedroom of the suite.

Seconds later she returned, her face pale. "It's gone, disappeared!"

"Not gone, Mrs. Hastings . . . taken," Carter said, and bolted from the suite.

As soon as he was on the street in the open, he got on the radio.

"Henderson!" he rasped several times as he ran to the waiting car. At last, through the static, Giles Henderson's voice came back to him.

"We've got both of them. They're moving in a roundabout way, but it looks like both of them are headed for the Eiffel Tower."

"It's a necklace," Carter hissed. "Dufont gave it to Mrs. Hastings in the cab on the way to Heathrow. It's missing. Chances are he's got it, and he's going to pass it."

"Got it," Henderson replied. "We're on 'em!"

● ● ●

Carter stood in the elevator operator's cubicle and surveyed the Parc du Champs de Mars below. The cubicle was on the third level of the Eiffel Tower, and afforded a perfect view of the whole park.

Lady Phyllis Loring sat on a bench in the park. She looked like a very chic Frenchwoman enjoying herself as she fed pigeons and chucked toddlers under the chin.

"Carter?"

"Yes?" he replied into the radio.

"Dufont is entering the park off Avenue de La Bourdonnais."

Carter shifted his glasses and immediately spotted the man striding purposefully toward the center of the quad. He swung an umbrella jauntily in his right hand and carried a newspaper clutched under his bicep against his left side.

Carter shifted the glasses back to the bench and the woman. And then he saw it, a paper, folded, by her side. He twisted the glasses to ultrahigh power and zeroed in on the paper. It was a London *Times*.

Interesting, he thought, in the Champs de Mars park, in Paris.

"Anybody!" Carter barked. "What's the paper under Dufont's arm? I can't spot it from up here!"

A heavily accented voice came back at once. "Monsieur, it is a London *Times*."

"Okay. Somewhere on the quad or in the park, somebody else has a London *Times*. Watch for it!"

By this time, Dufont had reached the bench. He stopped, lifted his shoe, and after setting his umbrella and the paper down, carefully retied the laces. This done, he picked up the umbrella and the woman's edition of the *Times*.

Not very original, Carter thought. But effective, since they didn't have to be too original at this stage of the game.

"He's coming out," said a voice on the radio.

"I know," Carter said. "Stay on him and don't lose him!"

"Should we pick him up?" Henderson asked.

"No, no way!" Carter barked. "I doubt if we have a

whole net here, but it's worth gambling for. Let me know if he heads back toward the George Cinq.''

''Monsieur Carter!''

''Yes?''

''Toward the top of the quad, heading toward the Tower, a woman. Tall, dark hair with streaks of gray, and dressed in a white skirt, sweater, and blouse.''

Carter moved the glasses again, quickly scanning the top of the quad. He spotted her in seconds. She had a paper under her arm.

''The paper, is it a *Times*?'' he hissed.

''*Oui, monsieur* . . . a London *Times*.''

Carter jiggled the glasses back and forth between the woman in white and Lady Phyllis Loring as they walked toward each other.

The exchange was professional, deftly done, with only a moment's hesitation. The papers were not traded. All Lady Phyllis did as she passed the other woman was tip her own newspaper. At the last second, a flashing object fell into the newspaper the woman in white held at her hip.

''It's made,'' Carter growled. ''Pick up the woman in white at the exit the moment she leaves the park. But first make sure she doesn't have a backup.''

For the next fifteen minutes, Carter sweated blood. And then the radio started and didn't stop.

''We have Dufont in a taxi on the motorway south out of Paris.''

''The Loring woman is also hailing a taxi.''

''Stay with her,'' Carter hissed. ''Are we clear on the woman in white?''

''*Oui, monsieur.*''

''Take her!'' Carter exclaimed, and darted out of the cubicle. He was taking the last flight three steps at a time, when the radio crackled again.

''Monsieur Carter . . .''

''Here!''

"We have apprehended the woman. She is a secretary in the Soviet embassy. She claims diplomatic immunity for anything we may charge her with."

"Do you have the necklace?"

"*Oui, monsieur.*"

"Then she can shove her diplomatic immunity up her ass. It's theft, and a British M.P. named Mildred Hastings will claim the necklace as soon as I can get her here."

"Nick?"

"Go ahead, Giles."

"They're both heading for Orly."

Carter's mind raced, and then he smiled. "Check the Aeroflot flights. I think they're going home."

Norman Dufont breathed a sigh of relief as he stepped through the last door and walked toward the huge white Aeroflot airplane.

Carla's dark head was already at the ladder, and he could see her above the others marching into the plane.

We've made it, he thought. *We've made it*.

A ground crewman nudged against him and slipped a piece of paper into his hands.

"*Urgent, monsieur,*" the man whispered, and quickly moved away.

Dufont flipped the paper open and glanced down. It said: *Look up. The observation deck.*

Carter stood with his arm around Mildred Hastings's shoulder. A bright sun gleamed down from the blue-domed sky, glinting off the shower of gold between her breasts.

"He looks very ill," she said.

"He has good reason to," Carter replied.

"You're letting them go?"

"We have no reason to keep them. And even if we did, the trial expense and the aftermath . . . why bother?"

She chuckled. "How right you are."

"Besides," Carter said, "neither one of them will fare very well in Moscow with this big a failure."

"Do you think they'll be executed?"

"Possibly. Or, at the very least, demoted to file clerks in an obscure Siberian village."

"Splendid," Mildred Hastings replied, lifting her hand and curling her fingers in a tiny wave. "So long, you bloody bastard."

DON'T MISS THE NEXT NEW
NICK CARTER SPY THRILLER

THE KILLING GROUND

On a clear day the ride up to the top of the Zugspitze was breathtaking. That morning the visibility was zero. Within a hundred feet of the cable house, the car was enveloped in a thick cloud, making it impossible to see anything but the gray, swirling mist.

A thousand feet up it began to snow, lightly, but in large flakes. If this kept up, Carter suspected they would close the lift. Too much snow made operating the cable car dangerous.

It was very cold at this altitude. Carter could see his breath.

A large tower suddenly loomed up, and they passed beside it, the pulleys bumping on the tower's tracks, then it was gone.

Carter lit a cigarette, then pulled out Wilhelmina and checked to make sure a round was in the firing chamber. He clicked the safety off as they passed another tower, and suddenly the mountain top came into view, a lone man standing on the broad veranda of the closed restaurant.

It was Ganin!

Carter looked for the latch that would open the cable car's window, noting Ganin's hand coming up. The Killmaster fell back into the corner of the car as the window glass was shattered. Two other shots whined off the side of the car before it slid into the upper terminal building.

For a few moments Ganin was out of sight. Carter leaped up on the inside handrails, flipped open the car's rooftop access hatch, and quickly pulled himself up, closing the hatch behind him.

He lay on his stomach as the car bumped to a halt. A second later Ganin came across the broad lobby from the veranda, and Carter snapped off two shots just as the car jerked beneath him. Both shots went wide and Ganin spun to the left, diving out of sight around the corner.

Carter rolled off the edge of the car, jumped down to the concrete platform, and leaped behind a steel support column, a single shot ricocheting off the steel inches from his head.

It was quiet in the building. Carter could hear the rising wind beginning to hum through the cables outside.

"You're not going to leave this mountain alive, Nick Carter!" Ganin called from around the corner.

"In that case you won't mind telling me where Lydia Borasova is being kept," Carter shouted.

Ganin laughed. "Are you in love . . . again, Carter? Haven't you learned your lesson?"

Carter said nothing.

"She is with Kobelev, in Innsbruck," Ganin said.

"Where in Innsbruck?"

"It does not matter, Carter."

"It matters to me, because after I kill you, I'm going to kill Kobelev," Carter said. He peered around the edge of the steel beam. There was a door at the rear of the cable car terminal that probably led back into the restaurant, or perhaps a storeroom.

There was silence in the lobby.

"Ganin?" Carter shouted. "It cannot hurt to tell me."

"They are stying in a chalet."

"Where?" Carter asked. He edged around the beam.

"At Axamer Lizum."

"Where the winter Olympics were held?"

"Yes, that is the place," Ganin said.

"Who else is with them?" Carter shouted, almost smiling; Ganin was so sure he would get Carter, he didn't think twice about giving him the information. He stepped around the beam and, keeping on the balls of his feet, raced to the rear door. It was unlocked.

"They are alone . . ." Ganin was saying as Carter slipped into a storeroom for the kitchen.

He raced down a narrow aisle, then through a set of swinging doors into the kitchen itself. From there he went out into the dining room, then hurried around to the front, and to the lobby.

Ganin was not there.

It took just a split second for Carter to realize that the Russian had probably come right behind him. He spun around the corner, bringing his Luger up, as Ganin came from the kitchen, the Russian's gun aimed at—Carter's chest.

Carter fired first, catching Ganin in the shoulder, shoving him backward into the kitchen.

Ganin fired twice as he fell, a hot stitch lacing into Carter's side, causing him to drop back.

The shot had been impossible, yet Ganin had missed killing Carter by less than two inches.

Carter watched the kitchen doors swing on their hinges for several moments before he slipped around the corner, and keeping low, he zigzagged to the wall beside the doorway.

There were no sounds from within the kitchen. Carter eased around the edge and looked through the window. The kitchen was empty. A trail of blood led across the white tile floor to a door on the opposite side of the room.

—From THE KILLING GROUND
A New Nick Carter Spy Thriller
From Charter in January 1986

☐ 74965-8	**SAN JUAN INFERNO**	$2.50
☐ 14222-2	**DEATH HAND PLAY**	$2.50
☐ 45520-4	**THE KREMLIN KILL**	$2.50
☐ 52276-9	**THE MAYAN CONNECTION**	$2.50
☐ 06861-8	**THE BLUE ICE AFFAIR**	$2.50
☐ 51353-0	**THE MACAO MASSACRE**	$2.50
☐ 69180-3	**PURSUIT OF THE EAGLE**	$2.50
☐ 24089-5	**LAST FLIGHT TO MOSCOW**	$2.50
☐ 86129-6	**THE VENGEANCE GAME**	$2.50
☐ 58612-0	**THE NORMANDY CODE**	$2.50
☐ 88568-3	**WHITE DEATH**	$2.50
☐ 03211-7	**THE ASSASSIN CONVENTION**	$2.50
☐ 06790-5	**BLOOD OF THE SCIMITAR**	$2.50
☐ 21877-6	**THE EXECUTION EXCHANGE**	$2.50

Prices may be slightly higher in Canada.

Bestselling Thrillers —
action-packed for a great read

__ $3.95 0-425-07671-7 **ROLE OF HONOR** John Gardner

__ $3.95 0-425-07657-1 **DAI-SHO** Marc Olden

__ $3.50 0-425-07324-6 **DAU** Ed Dodge

__ $3.95 0-425-08158-3 **RED SQUARE** Edward Topol and
Fridrikh Neznansky

__ $4.50 0-425-08383-7 **THE HUNT FOR RED OCTOBER**
Tom Clancy

__ $3.95 0-425-08301-2 **AIRSHIP NINE** Thomas H. Block

__ $3.95 0-441-37033-0 **IN HONOR BOUND**
Gerald Seymour

__ $3.95 0-441-01972-2 **AMERICAN REICH** Douglas Muir

__ $3.50 0-441-10550-5 **CIRCLE OF DECEIT**
Walter Winward

__ $3.50 0-441-27316-5 **GAME OF HONOR** Tom Lewis

__ $3.95 0-441-47128-5 **LAST MESSAGE TO BERLIN**
Philippe van Rjndt

__ $3.50 0-515-08337-2 **DEATHWATCH** Elleston Trevor

__ $3.95 0-515-08415-8 **QUILLER** Adam Hall

Prices may be slightly higher in Canada.